The airplane's engines exploded with exhaust and power, and it started going and going . . . and going. When it finally rose into the air, it did so very unsteadily, so much so that Aziz was certain it would slam right back into the ground. But somehow it stayed airborne and climbed painfully and slowly into the super-heated sky.

It was all too strange for Aziz; he just wanted to collect his fee and head back home.

Finally, the man he'd given the ride to came over to the side of the cab.

Aziz yelled down to him. "My fee, brother," he said. "And we'll be on our way."

The hitchhiker laughed and climbed up on the step so he was even with Aziz.

"I have something for you that is so much better than money," he told Aziz.

"And what can that be?" Aziz asked him.

The hitchhiker was suddenly holding a large handgun. He pointed it at Aziz's head and said, "Seventy-two virgins, of course."

Then he pulled the trigger.

Titles by Bill Kellan

STRIKEMASTERS
ROGUE WAR
FULCRUM

FULCRUM

BILL KELLAN

BERKLEY BOOKS, NEW YORK

THE BERKLEY PUBLISHING GROUP
Published by the Penguin Group
Penguin Group (USA) Inc.
375 Hudson Street, New York, New York 10014, USA
Penguin Group (Canada), 90 Eglinton Avenue East, Suite 700, Toronto, Ontario M4P 2Y3, Canada
(a division of Pearson Penguin Canada Inc.)
Penguin Books Ltd., 80 Strand, London WC2R 0RL, England
Penguin Group Ireland, 25 St. Stephen's Green, Dublin 2, Ireland (a division of Penguin Books Ltd.)
Penguin Group (Australia), 250 Camberwell Road, Camberwell, Victoria 3124, Australia
(a division of Pearson Australia Group Pty. Ltd.)
Penguin Books India Pvt. Ltd., 11 Community Centre, Panchsheel Park, New Delhi—110 017, India
Penguin Group (NZ), 67 Apollo Drive, Rosedale, North Shore 0632, New Zealand
(a division of Pearson New Zealand Ltd.)
Penguin Books (South Africa) (Pty.) Ltd., 24 Sturdee Avenue, Rosebank, Johannesburg 2196,
South Africa

Penguin Books Ltd., Registered Offices: 80 Strand, London WC2R 0RL, England

FULCRUM

A Berkley Book / published by arrangement with Kelcorp, Inc.

PRINTING HISTORY
Berkley mass-market edition / June 2010

Cover illustration by Ed Gallucci.
Interior text design by Kristin del Rosario.

For information, address: The Berkley Publishing Group,
a division of Penguin Group (USA) Inc.,
375 Hudson Street, New York, New York 10014.

ISBN: 978-0-425-22900-2

BERKLEY®
Berkley Books are published by The Berkley Publishing Group,
a division of Penguin Group (USA) Inc.,
375 Hudson Street, New York, New York 10014.
BERKLEY® is a registered trademark of Penguin Group (USA) Inc.
The "B" design is a trademark of Penguin Group (USA) Inc.

PRINTED IN THE UNITED STATES OF AMERICA

10 9 8 7 6 5 4 3 2 1

PART ONE

Gather enough ants together and they will bite an elephant to death.

—Chinese proverb

CHAPTER 1

Dasht-e Kavir
Central Iran

The three fuel trucks were hopelessly lost.

They were driving southeast on an ancient, unpaved road that was barely discernible from the desert around it. Flat, arid and arrow straight, the road seemed to go on forever. But the small convoy's destination, the oasis at al-Kareet, was nowhere in sight.

The lead driver, a man named Mahmoud Aziz, was having trouble reading his map—*that* was the problem. The map itself was hand-drawn and crude, and many of the directions seemed contradictory.

Each truck was pulling two thousand gallons of JP-8 aviation fuel, the kerosene-based propellant by which most jet airplanes flew. It was an odd cargo for Aziz and his men to be transporting. Normally they supplied diesel oil to various Iranian government buildings around the capital of Tehran, two hundred miles to the north.

That morning, though, his boss told him he'd be delivering the JP-8 to a new customer in a very unusual part of the country—the Dasht-e Kavir. Translated as the Great Salt Desert, it was Iran's version of Saudi Arabia's infamous Empty Quarter. Five hundred miles long by two hundred miles wide, there was nothing out here but quicksand, salt marshes, salt hills and the occasional mountain. It was so desolate, a similar area to the east, known as Dasht-e Lut, or Emptiness Desert, was brimming with life by comparison.

The desert fuel delivery would be four hundred miles round-trip. In return, Aziz's boss had promised his drivers an extra hour for lunch the following day. It had seemed like a good deal at the time, but now Aziz felt like the road they were following didn't end until the border of Afghanistan, which would surely mean they'd overshot their destination. More than once he considered turning around, though he knew his boss would be furious. Finally, though, after two hours of not knowing where they were, he decided it was time to return to Tehran and face the music.

It was strange, then, when just as he was about to signal his drivers to reverse direction, he saw a man up ahead flagging them down. Hitchhikers were a common sight in Iran; it was the regular mode of transportation for some people moving between cities.

But out here? In the middle of the hottest desert on Earth? The convoy was miles away from any human habitation, never mind a city. What was this man doing way out here?

Aziz decided to stop only because he hoped the hitchhiker might be able to tell them where they were—and get them going in the right direction. So began the process of downshifting and tapping the brakes for all three trucks. It took some finesse to bring six thousand gallons of jet fuel to a civilized halt.

The hitchhiker's face was covered by a kaffiyeh, and he was wearing jeans, sneakers and a T-shirt. Again, unusual for this part of the world. But he seemed friendly enough.

"*Salem alaikum*," he called up to Aziz once he'd stopped.

"Can you give me directions?" Aziz asked him in thick Farsi.

"Are you looking for the al-Kareet oasis?" the man asked in reply.

Aziz was surprised. "Do you know where it is?"

The man climbed into the truck's cab and said, "My brother, it's where I am going. It's just up the road."

THEY drove for another mile and around a rare bend in the road. The man pointed out a clutch of scrub trees, just about the only sign of vegetation amid all the salt. He told Aziz to turn east at the trees, off the road and onto the desert itself. Aziz did as the man said, followed by the two other tanker trucks.

Now they were heading for the base of a solitary mountain about a mile away. Built more of salt than dirt and rock, next to it was what appeared to be a grove of olive trees and mugwort plants surrounding a shimmering pool of water. But so much heat was rising off the desert floor, Aziz had to look closely, just to make sure it wasn't a mirage.

"It's real," his passenger assured him. "Of that, I'm certain."

And at first the hitchhiker seemed right. The closer they got to the oasis, the more things came into view for Aziz. The trees, the mugwort plants, the pool of water. A herd of goats was grazing on weedy grass inside an enclosure nearby. But the whole thing looked out of place for some reason. Nothing seemed natural. For instance, the oasis was located right up against the tall, sheer salt mountain, a very odd location.

But the strangest thing of all? Parked next to the oasis pool was a jet fighter.

Aziz was confused. He thought they were here to transfer the JP-8 from one set of tanker trucks to another. That's what his boss had led him to believe. So what was this jet doing way out here?

The three trucks pulled up to the oasis to find a small group of men standing around the airplane; they were dressed like the hitchhiker. Several trunks of heavy tools were nearby, as well as a network of fuel hoses. The men looked like skells to Aziz, a derogatory name for poor gypsylike Iranians who picked up scraps of metal and tin along desert roads and sold them to junk dealers.

Where the hell did they find a jet fighter? he thought.

He was no expert in these things, but Aziz knew the aircraft was definitely a warplane, one built to be flown by a lone pilot. He thought it might have been of Russian design. The airplane had no markings, though. Just a faded and peeling camouflage paint scheme.

The men standing around the airplane were visibly

relieved to see the trio of fuel trucks. No sooner had Aziz and his men pulled up than the skells were unfurling a pump hose to transfer the JP-8 from Aziz's truck directly to the airplane's tanks. More hoses were taken from the equipment trunks and soon the fuel from the other two trucks was being pumped across the oasis and into the side of the mountain itself, where storage containers must have been located.

Aziz and his men remained in their cabs and just watched the strange procedure. Aziz's attention was drawn back to the plane itself. One thing he noticed were heat waves rising from the rear of the aircraft. Was this just another illusion—or did it mean the plane had just flown here from somewhere else?

Also odd, the pilot, who was already strapped into the cockpit, wasn't wearing a flight suit or a crash helmet or even an oxygen mask. Instead he was wearing a kaffiyeh and sunglasses, covering his entire face. And he seemed to be holding a simple road map.

The fueling operation was completed quickly. The jet's engines were started up, causing many on hand to block their ears, yet oddly, Aziz noticed, not affecting the nearby herd of goats, which continued to graze peacefully. The group of men around the airplane had a long, shouted conversation with the pilot. They seemed to be giving him last-minute instructions. This, as other men were strapping boxes—*wooden* boxes—to the underside of the jet's wings, the place where bombs would normally be. One of the boxes was cracked open a bit, allowing Aziz to see its contents. To his surprise, the boxes contained sticks of dynamite.

How low-tech can you get? Aziz thought.

Finally, the group of men backed away, the pilot lowered his canopy and the plane started moving. There was none of the safety checks or precautions that usually accompanied the takeoff of a jet fighter. It simply rumbled away, engines screaming, toward a long straight patch of weeds that did not look at all like a typical runway.

Once in place, the airplane's engines exploded with exhaust and power, and it started going and going . . . and going. When it finally rose into the air, it did so very unsteadily, so much so that Aziz was certain it would slam right back into the ground. But somehow it stayed airborne and climbed painfully and slowly into the super-heated sky.

It was all too strange for Aziz; he just wanted to collect his fee and head back home.

Finally, the man he'd given the ride to came over to the side of the cab.

Aziz yelled down to him. "My fee, brother," he said. "And we'll be on our way."

The hitchhiker laughed and climbed up on the step so he was even with Aziz.

"I have something for you that is so much better than money," he told Aziz.

"And what can that be?" Aziz asked him.

The hitchhiker was suddenly holding a large handgun. He pointed it at Aziz's head and said, "Seventy-two virgins, of course."

Then he pulled the trigger.

* * *

Kuwait City
Thirty minutes later

More than five thousand people had joined the funeral procession.

Beginning at Rikkah and moving along the waterfront toward Sabah-as-salem, many of the participants were draped in black robes and headdresses and were flogging themselves or the person in front of them with small, mostly symbolic whips. The few women in the march wailed and whistled, but only at the direction of the procession's organizers, all of whom were carrying bullhorns so they could be heard above the throng. There were no soldiers or security troops in evidence. A few policemen were mixed in with the marchers, but none of them was armed.

At the head of the procession was a plain wooden coffin bearing Prince Ali Ahmed Rasif. An elderly member of the Kuwaiti royal family, Rasif had died of a heart attack while having sex with one of his fifty-five wives, a girl barely fourteen years old. One of the wealthiest men in the Persian Gulf, ironically Rasif had been roundly despised by the majority of Kuwaiti citizens. But theater was everything in this part of the world, so Rasif's family had promised each person marching in the procession a payment of $110 for an hour of their time. It was for this reason that most of the marchers were actually servants and civil workers, many of them not even Kuwaiti.

A few of the marchers, though, were as wealthy as Prince Rasif had been. Royalty from all over the Persian

Gulf were in the procession, as well as a few low-level diplomats from Europe and Africa. But probably the most unusual mourner was right up front, next to the coffin bearers, leading the way. He was Imam Ruhollah Rahstani. He was the sole representative from the Republic of Iran.

Rahstani held a powerful position within the group of theocrats that ruled Iran with an iron fist—but he also had a secret. Hoping to become the supreme leader of Iran someday soon, he'd been in contact with U.S. and European diplomats over the past few months. Always going through back channels, he'd been sending entreaties to them in hopes of establishing rapprochement between Iran and the West. Not only that, Rahstani had actually hinted that if he did rule Iran someday, he would take the huge step of recognizing the State of Israel.

As the procession moved toward the Qalm royal cemetery, the organized mourners began chanting Rasif's name. The sound of five thousand people shouting in unison became deafening. That's why very few people heard the jet fighter approaching.

It came out of the east, flying very low and unsteady over the water. Those who saw it at first thought it was a fly-by courtesy of the Kuwait air force, as another part of the memorial service. But when the plane went over the crowd low and fast, it was clear something was wrong.

After passing over the procession, the plane turned violently on its left wing and began heading back toward the cemetery. People started to panic now. Hundreds began running in all directions. But it was too late for most of them.

The plane slammed into the crowd, the crude wooden boxes of dynamite under its wings igniting on contact. It cartwheeled down the royal thoroughfare for more than a quarter mile, killing hundreds and setting many buildings on fire before finally coming to a stop.

In seconds, six city blocks were aflame, and hundreds lay dead in the street.

ONE figure emerged from the holocaust.

His clothes were burned completely off his body; his hair and beard were smoldering. Blood was running from his ears and mouth, and his right foot was broken. He was dragging something behind him, a piece of wreckage the size of a car battery. Painted bright orange, it was smoldering too. Between his teeth, he was carrying a credit card.

He staggered down an alley, fighting the tide of people running away from the fire and the chaos, and collapsed into a doorway. It looked like the entrance to a typical building in this part of the city, but the injured man, moving painfully, took the credit card from his teeth and slid it through an almost invisible slot next to the doorknob. The door opened, and the man fell in.

Two people were waiting on the other side to help him. He landed in their arms, barely conscious. One carried him up the long, elaborate stairway; the other carried the still-smoldering orange box. The stairway was the first sign this was not a typical building. Its walls were smooth and finished and well lit. It did not stink of sewage on the lower floors. Most of all, it was not stifling hot inside. The building was air-conditioned, top to bottom.

The building was also blast-proof and bomb-proof. Though the terrible conflagration had happened only three blocks away, and some of the surrounding structures were smoldering or damaged by the blast, this building was still standing and safe.

The burned man was carried to a room on the top floor of the building. The room was clean, cool and full of communications equipment.

Five more men were inside the room. Like the burned man, they were CIA operators. This was a safe house, one of many inside Kuwait City. These men were part of a U.S. cell tasked with spying on Iranian operatives known to be numerous in Kuwait. But today their assignment had been slightly different. Today, they were doing surveillance on an Iranian cleric who had been making overtures to the West in recent weeks and specifically was looking to make peace with the people of Israel.

Two men began attending to their injured colleague. His hands were horribly burned from carrying the smoldering orange box to the safe house. But he believed it was *that* important.

Bandages were applied to the wounds on his legs; his foot was put in a splint. Anti-infection medication was smeared on his burns and he was injected with a massive dose of morphine.

Only then was he able to talk.

"Rahstani's gone, he's dead," he was barely able to gasp. "He and a couple hundred other people."

"Some asshole planted a bomb," one man said. "Was it an IED or a car bomb? Could you tell?"

"It was not a bomb," the burn victim said emphatically. "I saw it come down."

The other men were confused. One was stationed at the window looking out on the carnage and fires three blocks away. There were still the vestiges of a small mushroom cloud rising over the site.

"If it wasn't a bomb, then what the hell was it?" he asked.

"It was an airplane," the injured man insisted.

"You mean an airplane crashed into the crowd?" another man asked. "What are the chances?"

"It wasn't an accident," the injured man said. "I saw it come down. It was a fighter plane. The pilot intentionally flew it right into the crowd."

The other men eyed each other. All were veterans of the wars of Southwest Asia and the Persian Gulf; they'd endured bomb blasts in practically every lawless city in the area. Indeed, they were almost daily occurrences for them.

The men were thinking the morphine was getting the best of their colleague. His job that day was to be a street man, an assignment each man in the cell had performed many times before. He'd been on the street not only to keep tabs on the pro-Western cleric but also to see who else was at the funeral march—known troublemakers or agents from other countries. That's when whatever happened happened. A bomb blast or some kind of trouble had not been unexpected.

But a plane crash didn't seem likely, never mind an intentional one. Though in the Persian Gulf these days, anything was possible.

The injured man's boots were just about the only thing that had not burned off him. He managed to reach inside one and pull out his cell phone.

It was not a typical Nokia—rather, the weapons experts at the CIA HQ in Langley, Virginia, had built it. It was the size and shape of a typical cell phone, but it was actually capable of functioning as a satellite phone. Plus its camera capability was outstanding.

"Play it," he said, feeling their skepticism. "See for yourself."

They did as he asked—and they were stunned. They could clearly see an aircraft appear above the funeral procession. And just as the street man had indicated, the plane flew low over the crowd, turned and then went into a screaming dive. It hit the front of the throng at about 500 mph and went end over end right down the procession route. Hundreds were incinerated immediately; hundreds more fled the area in flames.

It was like a vision from hell.

They ended the video—and contemplated what they had just seen.

"Look at the box," the injured man said.

They contemplated the orange box and quickly realized it was a flight data recorder, more commonly known as a black box. Made of virtually indestructible materials, these devices held information that could tell investigators what was going on just before a plane crashed. By extension, they also served as a way to identify the type and origin of the plane that carried it.

"This was from the airplane that crashed?" they asked the injured man.

He nodded painfully. "Find out where that came from," he said, "and you'll know who did this."

CHAPTER 2

New York City

Manhattan was hopelessly gridlocked.

From Harlem Heights to Battery Park, from the FDR Drive to the West Side Highway, no car, truck or bus was moving.

The bridges and tunnels were packed too. The subways had shut down because so many people had tried to use them to escape the city. Ambulances and emergency apparatus trying to navigate the monstrous traffic jam were blowing their sirens, adding to the confusion but going nowhere. The NYPD was desperate to get traffic flowing; a terrorist attack or a major fire under these conditions would have been catastrophic. But it was an impossible situation. The city was at a standstill—and incredibly, it had been like this for the past three days.

The cause of the traffic jam: Thousands of people, drawn here by viral messaging on the Internet, were in the streets demonstrating. Their message: The world was coming to an end and anyone who was a sinner better get straight with the Almighty now, before it was too late.

There was no denying that hints of the Apocalypse were everywhere lately. Global financial collapse seemed just one headline away. Nuclear tensions in the Middle East appeared past the boiling point. Drought was ravaging Africa. Food shortages were plaguing Asia. Epidemics. Pandemics. Important medicines in short supply. It was so bad that not only were individuals starting to hoard gold, but some big businesses were too.

Doom and gloom was the new fad and some people were *really* getting into it. Radical religious groups, many of them virulently antigovernment, were popping up all over the world, creating much of the noise that the end was near. The 24/7 worldwide media was covering the craze at a feverish pitch and what had been a drizzle of global maladies just a week before was now a tsunami of fear and paranoia. Nostradamus had been right, it seems; he was just a little bit off on his timing.

New York had become ground zero for these chaotic events. Street preachers were drawing huge crowds on just about every street corner of midtown. Thousands more had tried to storm the UN, Wall Street and even New York City Hall. Postcards were being distributed all over the city that had a place for recipients to enter their names and addresses next to a message that read: "If you don't see me around someday soon, then assume I've been 'raptured.'"

For those who didn't think they were going to make the cut when all the untainted souls rose into heaven, the number of people jumping off New York City's bridges had skyrocketed. It had become so bad, the NYPD had closed all pedestrian access to the spans and were heavily patrolling their walkways, trying to stop anyone from taking the plunge.

But they were fighting a losing battle. Suicides were up nearly 100 percent across the U.S. in just the past few weeks—and that number was increasing every day.

SITTING in a rented car in the middle of the chaos was U.S. Army colonel Doug Newman and an intelligence officer known as Lieutenant Moon.

Both were veterans of the U.S. Special Forces; both had seen a lot of combat. But neither had been as concerned for their safety as they were at this moment.

"These people are so pissed at the government they'd tear us to shreds if they knew who we were," the normally unflappable Moon said, trying to sink behind the steering wheel. He was a small man in his early forties, a slight ratlike look to his features. He always wore dark sunglasses and today was no different.

Riding in the passenger seat, Newman was older, bigger and more handsome. He bore a passing resemblance to John Wayne, if the iconic movie star wore a buzz cut and tattoos. Luckily both men were dressed in civilian clothes, hiding their military affiliation.

"I'll go down shooting," Newman replied to Moon's concern. He opened his briefcase to reveal an enormous Glock handgun with an extended ammo clip. It looked like a small cannon.

Moon studied the weapon. "Is that standard issue, Colonel?" he asked.

Newman almost laughed. "*Nothing* is standard issue these days," he replied.

Also in Newman's briefcase was a file marked "201—Current Status." Within its pages was a tale of top secret intrigue, black ops and the recent activities of a certain U.S. Special Forces unit so unauthorized simply having access to the file put one in danger of being court-martialed.

The file was Newman's major concern at the moment. He'd been aware of the anarchic problem in New York City back when they rented the car in Washington and began their drive up; after all, similar things were happening in big cities all across the country. But never did he think it would be *this* bad. People of all shapes, sizes and degrees of madness were banging on the car's windows, screaming at them to repent. How would Newman destroy the ultrasensitive file if the mob got in and, indeed, tore them to shreds?

The "201" stood for the 201st Special Operations Wing. At one time, Newman was its commanding officer. Birthed in the Nevada desert at a top secret training facility known as Area 153, the unit was formed a year before in response to a CIA study on worst-case scenarios the U.S. would face in the Middle East over the next ten years. Because the whole region was fragmenting so quickly, the CIA claimed the biggest threat would come from terrorist splinter groups run by a new type of religious fanatic called a warlord mullah. These people were envisioned as bloodthirsty, brutal, unreasonable holy men, in the spirit of al Qaeda, with plenty of money and access to weapons, including those of mass destruction. The CIA had identified at least a dozen of these warlord mullahs and was certain there would be more to come.

The Pentagon knew something had to be done about these mullahs, especially with all the other problems expected to pop up around the world in the next decade. So the 201st was put together as a large air-mobile assassination team that would identify and then eliminate these mullahs before they could start any trouble. It was a totally unconstitutional program—as well as a highly illegal way to head off a problem before it became a problem. *That's* why the 201st was so top secret from the start.

Ironically, though, the 201st never found any warlord mullahs to whack. Instead, it became entangled in two highly unauthorized missions—leaving the Pentagon with no other choice but to pull the plug. Newman just barely beat a life sentence at Leavenworth and the unit was ordered scattered to the winds. Any of its exotic ultra-tech equipment not destroyed during their brief controversial life span had been impounded by the government. All history of the 201st had been deleted from the Pentagon's main frames and all files concerning the unit had been expunged from the hard drives of those Washington insiders who formerly had a need to know.

Except for the information in Newman's briefcase, the unit had been erased—which turned out to be a big mistake.

Because suddenly it was needed more than ever.

This was why Newman and Moon were in New York. They were looking for the two principal officers of the super-secret special ops unit.

The rumor was they were holed up in a penthouse suite somewhere in Manhattan, making porn movies.

MAJOR Tommy Gunn opened his eyes to see the afternoon sunlight reflecting off an empty champagne bottle resting on the pillow beside him.

Through bleary pupils, he scanned his nearby surroundings. On the nightstand next to him three more empty bottles of Dom Perignon were competing for space with a big-screen TV remote, a tea saucer holding a few spoonfuls of a white crystal powder, a bong, a Digital8 camcorder, empty take-out food containers from an Iranian restaurant, a French restaurant and a Chinese restaurant and a half-eaten bagel. On the floor next to the bed, there were two sets of women's undergarments, a pair of fur-lined handcuffs, a whip, a pile of towels, and so many empty condom wrappers they were too numerous to count.

He closed his eyes again, and fell deeper in, recalling the weird dream he thought he just had. A crowd of people needing to get gas so they could all climb aboard a tiny plane and fly out of the desert. Or something like that. He turned over, his head pounding from the night before, and saw the most beautiful blonde in God's Creation lying next to him. She was naked, the sheets covering hardly anything at all. Breathing softly, she had a slight smile on her lips.

Gunn checked his pulse. He didn't think he was dreaming all this.

Then he reached over, picked up the hotel phone and dialed room service. "Could you send up some breakfast please?"

* * *

THE penthouse at the Novotel Hotel cost nine thousand dollars a night, gratuities not included. It boasted six bedrooms, three baths, a full bar, a living room, a media room, a wine room, an exercise room, a kitchen, a billiards room and a Jacuzzi the size of Lake Superior.

It also featured all-glass outer walls that allowed the occupants a 360-degree view of midtown Manhattan, including Times Square, Central Park and the Hudson River. On a clear day, one could see all the way into New Jersey.

Other, smaller top-floor suites were only slightly less expensive than this one; still, the hotel was full. Even though it was a cool spring day, Gunn could still hear his neighbors next door partying like it was New Year's Eve. He'd heard it was the same at just about every upscale hotel in Manhattan. Rambunctious behavior, lots of booze, lots of drugs, lots of women. Little interference from the authorities.

On a larger scale, the same thing was happening on the streets of the city, above and beyond the wacko demonstrations. The liquor was cheaper, the drugs not as pure, but the reason for the revelry was the same. These were not celebrations. They were preludes to a funeral.

They were called doomsday parties.

GUNN was an Air Force test pilot turned special operations commander. The beauty beside him was Lieutenant Amanda O'Rourke, a Navy fighter pilot who moonlighted as a magazine cover model.

They were the anomaly at the hotel. Their neighbors in the adjoining suites were mostly rap and hip-hop stars—like them, on hand to party like it was 1999, about ten years too late.

Gunn and Amanda could never have afforded this grand suite had they still been toiling under their military pay grades. But the last half year of their lives read like the script of an action movie—war, adventure, intrigue, lust. And through no fault of their own, they'd become stupid rich in the process.

They'd been the key officers for the 201st Special Operations Wing, the U.S. government's highly illegal assassination squad. To get away with whacking religious imams inside countries like Syria and Lebanon, the unit had been equipped with a company of 82nd Airborne paratroopers, a squad of Marine tanks and three C-17 Globemaster cargo jets specially converted into fearsome combat planes, one being an enormous gun ship sporting no fewer than sixteen weapons such as howitzers, field artillery pieces and Vulcan cannons.

But the C-17s also had another trick up their sleeves. They could become invisible. Not just on radar but, under the right conditions, to the naked eye as well.

The unit's first mission, a massive battle against an al Qaeda–affiliated group in Pakistan, resulted in the terrorists being overwhelmingly defeated. But the victory turned the 201st into a rogue unit as they had undertaken the operation without proper authorization.

The unit escaped to Africa, where it fought against those committing atrocities in the Sudan, then became embroiled in a massive search for nuclear terrorists roaming the African countryside looking for yellowcake uranium with which to make super-powerful nuclear bombs. As it turned out, the U.S. official who had sent them out on this search was in reality one of the world's most wanted terrorists—this was where the real-life action movie script came in—and as soon as they caught on, Gunn and Amanda pursued him, shooting down his plane and killing him before he could deliver a dirty bomb to the U.S. mainland.

For their trouble, Gunn and Amanda were given the fifty-million-dollar reward offered by the same U.S. government that had earlier ostracized them. And, of course, because he was Hollywood handsome and she was a cover model, they had become hopelessly romantic. With the 201st dispersed and their money stuffed inside some very creaky banks, they'd rented the top floor of the Novotel just in time to see the world go crazy below them.

THE knocking sounded a little too timid for room service. And Gunn doubted his new best friends, G-Zee and Un-Komin, were awake this early.

Still, he rolled out of bed, put on his blue silk robe and headed for the door. Breakfast these days was a magnum of champagne, two bowls of fruit and some coffee. He hadn't eaten since the previous afternoon—he'd been too busy doing other things—so he had a serious case of the munchies and needed food soon.

That's why he was so surprised when he opened the door to find neither the waiter nor the G-Pack but two other familiar faces standing on the other side.

"Colonel Newman?" Gunn asked. "Lieutenant Moon?"

Gunn thought he was tripping. These were the last two people he expected to see.

Newman scanned the expansive suite, noting the many empty liquor bottles and articles of women's lingerie strewn about. "Sorry to crash your party, Major. But we have to talk."

Gunn didn't know whether to salute or shake hands with Newman. The guy was his superior officer—the problem was, Gunn didn't know if he was still a member of the U.S. military or not.

At that moment, Amanda walked into the foyer. She'd thrown just a towel around her, so there was more skin showing than not.

Newman and Moon froze at the sight of her. She was as surprised to see them as they were entranced by her. She almost snapped off a salute too, but it didn't seem appropriate, plus the towel would have fallen to the floor. So she quickly excused herself and disappeared back into the bedroom. That's when the room service arrived.

Newman and Moon came in with the food cart. Gunn tipped the server and he departed. Then Gunn invited the two officers to sit in the living room.

He was surprised when both officers accepted his offer for a glass of champagne. He poured himself a glass and they did a quick, perfunctory toast.

"So," Gunn said. "You tracked us down. Should I even ask why?"

Moon opened his laptop and activated the screen. It

showed a line of elderly jet fighters at some unidentified air base. The aircraft were of Russian and French design. They wore no country insignia, no aircraft ID numbers. They looked in woeful need of maintenance.

"Recognize these bad boys?" Newman asked Gunn.

Amanda had joined them at this point. She'd put on one of Gunn's dress shirts but still looked extra sexy. It was hard for her not to.

"That's what used to be the Iraq Air Force circa 1991," she said, sitting down and studying the airplanes. "Which means that picture was taken somewhere in Iran."

It sounded upside down, but she was right. At the beginning of the first Gulf War, most of the Iraqi Air Force inexplicably fled next door to archenemy Iran to avoid the Coalition onslaught. The fleeing aircraft included French-built Mirage F-1s, Russian-built Su-17s and Su-20s, plus MiG-21s, MiG-25s and the most dangerous, MiG-29 Fulcrums. More than 130 planes in all jumped over the border to Persia.

The Iraqi pilots were interned and after a while quietly released. But for a long time, most of their warplanes sat idle. At the time, the Iranians were having trouble getting their own air force off the ground. It consisted mostly of U.S.-built F-14 Tomcats sold to the country before the Islamic Revolution. Chronically short of parts, the Iranians worked hard just to keep a handful of their Tomcats flying. Though they tried to incorporate some of the ex-Iraqi aircraft into their own air force, to suddenly have these French and Russian airplanes drop out of the sky on them was more a curse than a blessing.

"Why are you showing us this?" Gunn asked. "I thought most of those planes were rust and dust long ago?"

"Well, they were," Newman said. "Until recently."

He signaled Moon to go to the next image. It showed a still shot of a street in what was identified as downtown Kuwait City. Everything within the picture frame was engulfed in flames. Six blocks of buildings, vehicles and people in the process of being immolated.

Most noticeable, in the middle of the photo was what was obviously the wreckage of an aircraft. It was about the size of a MiG-21.

"One of them was shot down?" Amanda asked. "Over Kuwait?"

Newman and Moon shook their heads.

"No," Newman replied. "One of them *crashed* in the middle of that crowded street—on purpose."

It took a moment for Gunn and Amanda to let this sink in.

"'On purpose?'" Amanda said. "You mean like a suicide attack?"

Newman nodded grimly. "There was a funeral procession in progress down that street. Whoever was flying that airplane knew that—and purposely plowed right into it."

Gunn studied the photo closely. "Any way it was just a terrible coincidence?"

Newman shook his head no. "Many witnesses saw the plane circle around before it went in. The pilot was looking for a target. And he found it . . ."

"And we're sure it was one of the old Iraqi planes?" Gunn asked.

Another image came up on Moon's screen. It showed a small piece of burned wreckage, painted orange.

"This is the black box from the airplane," Newman explained. "One of our CIA brothers recovered it from the street right after the crash—and burned half the skin off his hands in the process. The box wasn't working at the time of the crash, but we traced it back to Iraq in 1991, and to the MiG factory in Russia before that. There's no doubt about it. It came from one of those ex-Iraqi planes. But there's more . . ."

Moon flipped to another image. It showed the wreckage of what looked to be a pair of planes burning in the desert.

"That's a Gulfstream—or what's left of it—near the Iran–Iraq border," Newman said. "And that's also the remains of another MiG-21. This happened less than twelve hours ago."

Newman looked around the big suite. "You guys haven't had the TV on?" he said.

Gunn and Amanda eyed each other sheepishly. "Not the regular channels," she replied softly.

"Well, the media is reporting this as strictly an airplane accident," Newman said. "But we know that the MiG-21 intentionally hit that Gulfstream in midair."

Moon flipped to another image. It showed three separate photos, side by side: one of a palatial estate engulfed in flames, another looked to be a midsized cruise liner smoking heavily and sinking, and the third was of a mosque somewhere in the Middle East, also in flames. In all three, the wreckage of a jet fighter was prominent in the image.

•

"These all happened in the last twenty-four hours too," Newman said. "They all occurred inside Iran, so they're keeping the lid on them. But they're all definitely the same MO."

"MY God." Amanda gasped. "So there's a new kind of suicide bomber going round? One that uses jet airplanes? Is that what you're saying?"

Both Newman and Moon nodded grimly.

"As far as we can tell," Newman confirmed. "Though, truthfully, no one is exactly sure what's going on. The funeral procession the first plane plowed into was being led by a highly placed Iranian cleric named Rahstani. He'd been making overtures to the West lately and had even talked about discussing a peace agreement with Israel."

"You're kidding," Gunn said. "Those two countries are sworn enemies."

Newman just shrugged. "Well, this guy was trying to change that. As was a guy on that Gulfstream, the guy on that yacht, the guy in the mansion and the guy who was preaching in that mosque. They were all what we would call moderate Iranians and they were all allies of this Rahstani guy. And now they're all dead—killed the same way, by a suicide plane connected with those ex-Iraqi fighters that wound up in Iran. We got the four other black boxes to prove it."

"So, what's the prevailing theory?" Gunn asked.

Moon shrugged. "That a very radical sect of the Iranian military found out about Rahstani's entreaties, secretly refitted some of those ex-Iraqi airplanes and used them on suicide missions to stamp out the peace feeler movement in a very visible way."

"But what do the Iranians say about all this?" Amanda asked.

"They're denying it, of course," Moon replied. "But, on background, we've picked up some chatter that indicates they're as shocked and surprised as we are that these things are happening. Those ex-Iraqi airplanes fell out of their control in the past few months. No one is sure why, but they were supposed to be stripped down and sold for scrap—that is if anyone in that country really knew how to do those types of things. But, again, through indirect channels we are hearing the Iranians have no idea what's going on either. They don't know who is responsible or even where the ex-Iraqi planes are at the moment, never mind where they're taking off from. It's all very scary . . ."

"And it gets worse," Newman interjected. "Our friends at the CIA think that these initial attacks might just be the beginning."

"The 'beginning' of what?" Gunn asked.

"They feel because this seems to be an anti-Israeli thing that the real attacks are eventually going to be on Israeli targets—and that this is just a warm-up," Newman said. "A major city. A military base. Even the Israeli nuclear facility at Dimona. That's the current thinking. And some people are even floating rumors that whoever has these airplanes might have a couple nukes to put on them eventually. Now, you know things like this drive the Israelis nuts. And though they have some of the best early-warning systems on the planet, nothing is impossible. And if just one of those suicide planes ever gets through to Jerusalem or Tel Aviv or someplace, well . . ."

Gunn almost laughed at this. "But wait a minute," he said. "If we know all this, then I'm sure the Israelis know it too. And they ain't gonna let any of that stuff happen. They'll blow the crap out of Iran in a . . ."

That's when he stopped and realized what he was saying.

"Exactly," Newman said. "The Israelis will rain destruction on Iran—most likely with nukes. But you know what happens then?"

"Hezbollah, which we believe has small nukes of its own, will attack Israel with them, at the behest of Iran," Moon said. "So then Israel will counterattack Hezbollah, which means Lebanon, again maybe with tactical nukes. All the other Muslim countries in the region will then be obligated to go in against Israel—that means Pakistan with its nukes, and that means India will probably attack Pakistan, and that means Russia or China will probably attack India, because we've found out both have secret treaties with Pakistan, and that means we'll have to attack China or Russia and they'll have to attack us. And what you'll have then . . ."

"Is what all those people out in the streets are screaming about." Amanda finished the sentence for him. "Armageddon. The final battle. The end of the world."

"Exactly," Newman said. "And I have some strong contacts in Israel—especially in their intelligence service. And they are telling me they are not waiting around for this one. They are absolutely going to launch a preemptive strike on Iran because of this. It's just a matter of time. And when they do, it will tip over all those dominoes."

A grim silence came upon the room.

"Damn," Gunn said. "So, the 'end *is* near.' "

"It looks that way," Newman said. "Unless we can do something about it."

"Which is?" Amanda asked, gripping Gunn's hand.

"The Israelis have given us a time frame," Newman said. "Just like in the first Gulf War when Saddam was firing Scuds at them. They agreed to hold off entering the war if we were able to go in and kill the Scuds. For the most part, that's what happened—although the war ending so quickly was the real reason that threat passed. But if you recall, the Israelis had their fighter bombers out on the runways, charged up, and ready to go. That's exactly what's happening over there right now—except this time, those fighter bombers are armed with nukes.

"So what we have to do is find the rest of these suicide jets and whack them before they can carry out their plans. Or find the brains behind the attacks and whack them—and put an end to it that way. Most likely what we got to do is do both things—and even then it might not be enough to avoid the sky from falling in."

Gunn's head was swimming—both from this devastating news and the champagne. It was all so dreamlike.

"What's the Israelis' time frame?" he asked. "I can't imagine them staying patient very long. After a couple weeks they'll be chomping at the bit to go."

Both Newman and Moon laughed darkly. "In *a week*

there's a good chance none of us will be here," Newman said. "The time frame is forty-eight hours and the clock started ticking at seven this morning, our time."

Both Gunn and Amanda were stunned.

"But what do they expect *us* to do?" Amanda asked. "The unit was dissolved after our African 'vacation.' All of our equipment is gone. The planes, the tanks."

For the first time, Newman actually smiled. He looked at Moon who had his BlackBerry out and was madly punching in numbers.

"Pack whatever you can inside of five minutes," he said. "We've got to get going."

"What do you mean?" Gunn asked.

"I mean we're putting the unit back together," Newman said bluntly. "Among other things."

"You guys are kidding," Gunn said, almost in a gasp.

Moon drained his glass and poured himself another. "Major—do you really think we'd fight our way through that madhouse down there just for a gag?"

Newman also topped off his glass. "The lieutenant is correct," he said. "We have a very serious problem and the NSC is gathering together every special ops group in existence—and even a few that aren't. They are that desperate. So we got the call. So let's get moving. And that's an order."

EXACTLY five minutes later, Gunn and Amanda, each with a backpack in hand, were walking out of the penthouse. They could still see the chaos in the streets below and couldn't believe they'd be able to go anywhere in the mess.

But Newman and Moon did not lead them to the elevator. Rather they took a short stairway up to the roof of the hotel.

Waiting for them up here was a V-22 Osprey, the half plane, half helicopter flown by the Marine Corps.

But this craft was no ordinary V-22. It was painted in dull, almost sinister black camouflage. It had more antennas and communication masts sticking out of it than a weather station. It was also almost perfectly silent despite the two huge rotors spinning at the end of its stubby wings.

As it turned out some of the hotel's other guests were up on the roof. G-Zee, Un-Komin and a host of others were having a smoke and enjoying the late afternoon sun. They were very impressed by Gunn and Amanda's new ride and told them so.

Gunn and Amanda piled into the Osprey, followed by Newman and Moon. The V-22's crew were wearing uniforms of the TF-160 Nightstalkers, the Army's most elite chopper group. No sooner was the access door closed than the unusual aircraft rose into the sky, G-Zee and his posse cheering as it ascended.

Gunn and Amanda looked out the window of the V-22 as it started its flight over midtown Manhattan. Theirs was a view of the chaos below on a grand scale. Not only was every street filled with surging crowds, they could also see some of the crowds were now engaged in running battles with the police. There were scattered fires flaring up throughout midtown, but of course the fire apparatus couldn't get to them.

There were also large numbers of police on the bridges leading out of the city. Many people were jumping off the spans, and the police were scrambling up and down the bridges' walkways, trying to pull people from the railings.

The entire scene was one of pandemonium—even by New York City standards.

Amanda squeezed Gunn's arm as the city faded from view.

"Maybe this is a party that we *should* miss," she said.

CHAPTER 3

THE V-22 headed south.

Not fifteen minutes later, Gunn and Amanda were flying over a heavily wooded part of New Jersey known as the Pine Barrens. This was a very weird place. Isolated, unsettled and uncivilized, it was one million acres of thick forest and impossibly dense undergrowth that covered a large part of the tollbooth state.

There was a mist blanketing one section of this oddly placed wilderness. Gunn thought this strange as it had been a clear, sunny day when the V-22 left New York City just minutes before. Amanda noticed it too.

"They get different weather in New Jersey?" she asked him.

Gunn saw Newman and Moon looking out at the fog bank, but they remained silent. So it was no great surprise that the Osprey headed right for this weird cloud of mist. Once over it, the V-22 did a sharp bank and started descending rapidly. For one brief moment, Gunn thought the tilt-wing plane was in trouble. The hybrid aircraft was not exactly a five-star safety award winner. The tops of the trees were coming up very quickly at them.

But then Amanda said two words: "Electronic camo."

He knew what she meant right away. They were looking down not on a "real" forest, at least not directly below them, but rather on an enormous sheet of futuristic camouflage, the same type of which covered the 201st's training base in Nevada. The camouflage cover was actually a mosaic of electromagnetic images taken of the surrounding terrain and printed on top of one another like photographs. By overlaying thousands of these images, a realistic impression of what would be here, on this piece of ground below them, was created. The illusion produced by the covering was so realistic the ruse was only apparent to someone who was standing right up next to it.

A hole in the net opened now and the V-22, transformed into its vertical mode, slowly descended through it. And incredibly, below the camo netting was an air base. It was about a half mile square and contained one long runway. Gunn and Amanda were astonished. This place was just a stone's throw from Manhattan and even closer to the dense populations of Philadelphia and Atlantic City. Yet here it was, a secret government base, right under a few million noses.

The base was not only surrounded by trees and dense overgrowth, but many patches of flora remained inside the facility as well. The runway was on the eastern end of the base; a half-dozen hangars ran alongside it. All these buildings were covered with the exotic electromagnetic camouflaged netting too. Add in the patches of remaining overgrowth and trees and the buildings could hardly be seen at all.

The V-22 landed with a bump. Rolling up to the edge of the taxiway, Gunn and Amanda saw no lights, no people, no signs of life at all. There was just grayness and the fog. A lot of it . . .

The V-22 pilots steered the aircraft right up to one of the hangars; it was the largest structure on the base. It was clear that camo netting or not, the V-22 pilots wanted to get out of sight as quickly as possible. The hangar door opened and the V-22 rolled inside. When the door closed, it was as dark as night within the huge aircraft barn.

Newman and Moon climbed out of the V-22; Gunn and Amanda were close behind. Suddenly they heard the most unexpected noise: applause. It was only then that they realized there were more people inside the hangar. A light was turned on and Gunn began seeing faces—familiar faces.

Pilots. Gunners. Paratroopers. Marines. Ground support people. They were lined up in a ragged assembly.

It was the 201st—their old unit.

They were applauding at the appearance of Gunn and Amanda, their two senior pilots.

One man walked out of the crowd. It was Lieutenant George "Bada" Bing, their close friend.

They shook hands with him. "Welcome back," was all he said.

Newman and Moon hurried Gunn and Amanda to the front line of the assembled troops. There were about 120 people in all. Then, out of the shadows, three officers appeared. Gunn didn't recognize them, but he knew by their uniforms that they were generals. One was Army, one was Marine, and the third was Air Force.

Two men in civilian clothes were with them. It was easy to tell who these guys were: CIA spooks. They were hard to miss.

The five men practically ran to a spot facing the assembly. The Army general produced a single piece of yellow paper. In the special ops business, yellow paper usually meant something important—and this time was no exception.

The senior officer began reading from the paper but was doing so in such a hasty fashion neither Gunn nor anyone else could make out all of what he was saying. But they were able to hear key words, and that's all that mattered. Words like: "Past missions may have been overextended" and "Some orders may have been misinterpreted." And: "The book is closed on these missions" and "The unit as a whole deserves recognition."

The last sentence was the most important, though, and everyone in the building heard it clearly: "As of this date, by order of the President of the United States, the 201st Special Operations Wing is hereby reactivated."

The general looked out at the assembly and said, "Carry on and good luck."

With that, the brass and the spooks departed as quickly as they appeared.

Newman took their place and said: "OK, fun's over. Let's move out. We have a long trip ahead of us."

With that, everyone started jogging out of the big hangar and heading for the two air barns next door.

Newman quickly led Gunn and Amanda to the next hangar over. Here, they saw yet another old friend. It was the C-17 that everyone in the unit called Heavy Metal. It was the plane that had carried the 201st's pair of Marine Corps tanks in their previous actions. It was also the only one of the unit's trio of "invisible" airplanes to survive their African adventure.

Heavy Metal had been Amanda's plane; she'd flown it into battle, perfecting the technique of landing on short, rough runways and releasing the pair of M1-A1 tanks in a matter of seconds. She walked up to the plane now and stroked the fuselage as if she was patting a horse.

But Heavy Metal looked different; it had obviously been refitted as a gunship. Like Gunn's earlier plane, it now boasted sixteen weapons, all installed in bays cut out of the port side of the fuselage. Miniguns, cannons, artillery pieces, even howitzers, it was the same idea as an AC-130 Spectre gunship, except with four times more firepower.

"We were critically short on time, so we had to improvise," Newman explained. "So your old tank plane is now three planes rolled into one. It still carries the tanks, it has enough room for the paratroopers and it's now a gunship as well."

Gunn was stunned. "Are you saying we're *all* going in this?" he asked Newman.

Newman replied, "Most of you are."

He led them to the next hangar over. He opened the door and both Gunn and Amanda let out a gasp.

Before them was another C-17. It was dull black, just like Heavy Metal, but it was obviously a new airframe, fresh off the assembly line. And something else was different. This plane had two turrets on it—one in the nose, one on top of the fuselage behind the flight deck. Turrets were something not seen on an American aircraft since the 1950s.

"Are you expecting the Luftwaffe to intervene?" Gunn asked Newman, puzzled.

"Them we could handle," Newman replied dryly. "But no—those turrets aren't for twin-fifties. Take a closer look."

Gunn and Amanda approached the huge airplane and studied the nose turret. It resembled a twenty-first-century version of an old B-17 turret: a movable Plexiglas-enclosed bubble with two barrels sticking out of it.

But like Newman said, these weapons were hardly the twin .50-caliber machine guns used by valiant air force gunners to shoot down German interceptors over war-ravaged Europe. They looked like weapons built for the next century, not the previous one. They were actually glass tubes, each about three feet long and three inches in diameter. Slightly purple in color, they had an odd glow to them. They were connected to a box inside the turret that was surrounded by so many wires they resembled high-tech spaghetti.

There was a trigger assembly of sorts—the gunner had a small HUD screen with which to spot the target. A lever activated the weapons.

But what were they exactly?

"Chemical oxygen iodine lasers," Newman answered before they could even ask the question. "COILs for short. Dangerous high-energy weapons—with a range that's strictly classified. What you see here just in this turret was once so big it filled a 747. But they've managed to shrink it down to this size and install a suitable power supply inside the airplane as well."

"And what are you expecting to use them for?" Gunn asked.

"Well, that's the crux of the mission," Newman told them. "This plane is being deployed, along with many other special operations forces' assets, in the hope that they can find and shoot down any Iranian suicide planes before they can get to Israel itself—and we have Armageddon on our hands. We're hoping these lasers can solve a very big problem for us."

Gunn looked back at the three-in-one plane. Most of the 201st had already loaded aboard: paratroopers, Marines, and their two tanks.

"But what are we going to do?" he asked Newman.

The senior officer checked his watch. "I'm hoping we find out when we get to the next stop," he replied quickly. "But for now we've just got to get the hell out of here. Our doomsday time frame is down to less than forty hours."

While the three-in-one plane was fully loaded, only about a dozen people were climbing into the laser-equipped plane. One of them was Bada Bing. The rest were civilians, or at least people dressed in civilian clothes.

"This is your ship?" Gunn asked Bing as he walked by.

"That's what they tell me," Bing said. It was clear that he was not thrilled with his new assignment.

"And who are these guys?" Gunn asked, eyeing the civilians climbing aboard the new plane. "Covert CIA?"

Bing laughed grimly. "They're company reps," he replied. "They're employees of the company that made the lasers. What they tell me is they're not even sure these freaking things work."

Gunn looked back at him—he really didn't know what to say.

Finally, he was able to blurt out, "But what about you—and this new plane. Do you know how to fly it with all this new stuff on board?"

Bing just shrugged. "Nope," he said. "Not yet . . ."

With that, he gave Gunn a quick salute and then disappeared up into the new C-17, Newman on his tail.

At that moment, Gunn heard a strange sound—like that of rushing air or steam. Not a jet engine noise but some kind of propulsion system.

He rejoined Amanda and they both turned to see a very strange aircraft descending into the base. It was not a V-22 Osprey, but that was the closest thing it resembled. It was about the size of a small airliner and had movable wings like a V-22. But instead of huge proprotors, it had very unusual jet engines—or something like jet engines—on its tips.

Gunn had been in the military flying business for years—so had Amanda. They'd seen some strange things flying around when they were assigned to Area 153 out in the middle of the Nevada desert.

But they had never seen anything like this.

As they watched, Lieutenant Moon walked out onto the tarmac and prepared to climb into the strange aircraft. Before he did so, he turned and looked at Gunn and Amanda standing about a hundred feet away. For the first time either of them could remember, Moon was not wearing his trademark wraparound Bono-style sunglasses. To their surprise, his eyes belied his slightly rattish facial features. They were large and soft, not small and beady. And at the moment, they were filled with concern. Normally ice-cold cool, Moon actually looked worried.

He waved to them, sadly, then finally climbed into the strange aircraft. It began to rise even before the access door was closed. It shot straight up through the hole in the electronic camo net, to a spot over the base. Then its movable power plants were spun forward—and the aircraft was suddenly gone, just like that.

Gunn and Amanda were astonished.

"What the hell was that thing?" Gunn asked.

Amanda could only shrug. "I have no idea," she said.

Gunn turned to look at her—and now she appeared very worried too.

"What's the matter?" he asked her, her eyes still skyward.

"I don't know," she said. "It's just that we've been through a lot with that guy. He's saved our butts more than once."

"And?"

Amanda moved a little closer to Gunn.

"And for some reason," she said, "I'm not sure we're ever going to see him again."

THE pair of C-17s took off just after sunset. Both employed their wing-mounted rocket assists to get them off the ground with a take-off roll of less than five hundred feet. The rockets lifted them up through the hole in the rolled back camouflage netting before finally shutting down. As soon as the pair both cleared the tops of the pine trees, the camouflage netting rolled itself back into place and the hidden base was hidden once again.

But that's when the huge planes employed their most fantastic secret weapon of all.

They became invisible.

It wasn't as impossible as it sounded. For the most part, the 201st's aircraft were typical C-17 Globemaster cargo planes; they just happened to be loaded with some very untypical technologies. Considered the workhorse of the U.S. Air Force in its role of moving Army troops around the world, a standard C-17 looked like an airliner on steroids. At 175 feet long and a wingspan of almost the same length, these planes could fly anywhere on Earth in just a matter of hours, in any kind of weather, day or night, land on rough, unprepared surfaces, unload their cargo and then take off the same way.

What made the 201st's C-17s so different started with their skin—or, more accurately, their "Star Skin." Each plane was painted in dull, nonreflective black, and embedded in this paint was a matrix of tiny twinkling sensors, tens of millions of them. These sensors could detect stars, star formations, clouds, atmospherics or any mix thereof that appeared above the aircraft and re-create them exactly onto its bottom. As such, the aircraft, which were also equipped with silent engines and other stealth technologies, could pass overhead at night and not be seen by anyone on the ground because what they thought they were looking up at was nothing but the stars. In other words, under the right conditions, they could indeed become invisible.

This was how the two planes made their way through the crowded New York–New Jersey air corridor undetected.

Once out over the Atlantic, they turned east.

GUNN stayed in the copilot's seat for all of this. Though the Heavy Metal plane had been extensively modified, he still considered it Amanda's aircraft. It was hers to command.

Plus, as she was doing the flying, it allowed him to inspect the new three-in-one plane. Again, just like his old C-17, the new Heavy Metal gunship carried sixteen massive weapons. And just like his old plane, the inside of its enormous cargo bay looked like a nightmare of ammo belts, power lines and gun muzzles, now with two huge M1-A1 tanks and several dozen fully equipped paratroopers squeezed in as well. But there was method to the madness, at least to the educated eye. Starting from the rear of the plane, the first weapons were a pair of M102 105mm howitzers, a field gun that had been used by the U.S. Army for years. Next was a trio of 20mm M61Vulcan cannons. Not unlike those installed on F-15 and F-16 jet fighters, they could each fire three thousand rounds a minute. Following the Vulcans were four Mk-44 Bushmaster 30mm cannons—long, scary-looking weapons that fired air burst rounds. Next to the Bushmasters were four 7.62mm GAU-2/miniguns. They could fire at *four thousand* rounds a minute, and were usually loaded with incendiary rounds. Next came a pair of 40mm Bofors cannons, extremely high-powered anti-aircraft guns adapted for airborne use.

The last weapon in this murderer's row was the fiercest one of all: a Phoenix CIWS gun. This was a monstrous Gatling gun more readily used to protect capital naval ships like aircraft carriers and cruisers. It was radar-directed, with six barrels, and fired a 20mm shell. It could also fire four thousand rounds per minute over a very large area. It was able to throw out so much lead, so quickly, nothing in its path could escape.

All this firepower was directed through gun stations cut into the left side of the aircraft and controlled by the pilot via an LCD screen. Installed just above the flight computer, this screen displayed icons for each weapon. Once the pilot was ready to unload on something, the weapon of choice could be selected by touching the weapon's icon. Push the activate panel and the fire control computer did the rest.

Gunn was the first to admit the number of weapons on board was almost overwhelming. In its first real combat action, his original gunship had taken the top off a twelve-thousand-foot peak in Pakistan simply by firing all of its guns at once. So, was there such a thing as *too much* firepower? The crew of this new hybrid was certainly in a position to find out.

ABOUT an hour into their flight, Amanda suggested Gunn get some sleep. He looked terrible and she didn't mind telling him so. They were flying into the night, at about forty-five thousand feet, the C-17's four big engines going full out. All was OK, at least for the moment—but could he really go to sleep? With every breath, with every passing minute, the urgency of what was going on in the world seemed to go up another notch. Not ideal conditions for a good night's rest.

Nevertheless, Gunn did retire to one of the pull-down seats just behind the flight deck. He was still battling a hangover, and everything still seemed like it was a bad dream. He stared out the tiny window next to the seat, first looking back toward the west, as the last of the North American landmass slipped away into a dark, bloodred sky and then forward, to the inky black night ahead. A chill went through him. Suddenly, it *looked* like the end of the world.

Gunn slipped into a kind of stupor—not quite sleep, as he felt like he was already asleep. And he saw things as if from a dream, but not quite, as he felt he was already dreaming. He wondered what effect all the things he'd ingested over the past few weeks was having on him—but at one point he was looking out the window and saw the shape of a B-52 bomber pass overhead, maybe twenty-five hundred feet above them. It was going much faster than they, which was weird because the B-52 and the C-17 had just about the same top speed, just a bit under 600 knots.

Another time he thought he saw a formation of F-22 fighters pull up right alongside the gunship. Except these were not normal Raptors. They too were wearing their Star Skin—and he saw them only as silhouettes against the star-studded sky. But if this had really happened, then how could he have seen the odd F-22s at all?

Weirdest of all, though, he thought he saw dozens of

B-2 Stealth bombers streak by them. Again, they were going faster than they should have been. In fact, they looked like a huge flock of mechanical geese, flying in a rigid chevron.

From somewhere deep in Gunn's groggy mind, a question popped out.

Why would anyone be in a hurry to get to Armageddon?

PART TWO

CHAPTER 4

THE spare crowd visiting the Persepolis suddenly saw a small army of national police descending on the ancient ruins.

There were just a couple dozen sightseers looking over the famous three-thousand-year-old Persian Empire site—amateur German photographers mostly—here to take photos of the ruins at night.

Their tour bus had brought them here just forty-five minutes before—and the post-midnight tour of the site was supposed to last three hours. But now the police were making it quite clear that they wanted the site cleared and quickly. For emphasis, they were waving their guns and nightsticks around.

The German tourists quickly obeyed. They weren't bothered so much, as the skies had become thick with black rain clouds. A massive thunderstorm was about to open up right above the ancient site.

Within ten minutes, the tourists and the bus were gone. The police waited and searched the site one more time and, satisfied that it was empty, soon left as well. Within fifteen minutes, there wasn't anyone within twenty miles of the isolated ruins.

Soon enough, a loud crack was heard coming out of the sky. Off in the distance, a helicopter was approaching. It was a worn-out, French-built Gazelle. It circled the site once and then set down near the southeast edge of the ruins.

One man climbed out and the helicopter departed as quickly as it came. He was Colonel Sharif Shabiz, deputy commander, Ministry of Intelligence and Security. Better known as the MOIS, it was the Iranian government's much-feared intelligence service.

Shabiz looked up into the dark sky. He was in his midfifties, paunchy and overweight. He felt uncomfortable without his uniform on. The civilian clothes he was wearing just didn't fit right.

Maybe this is a trap, he thought.

In the next moment, another clap of thunder shook the ruins—or at least it *sounded* like a clap of thunder. Shabiz saw the dark clouds overhead part, and a large, very strange-looking aircraft begin to descend out of them.

A chill ran through him. This thing, with its odd shape and movable wings and weird propulsion tubes on its wingtips, and its strange bubble cockpit, looked like something from the ancient Persian texts about huge war machines that flew on the wings of gods and could lay waste to vast stretches of land in one fell swoop.

"Fucking Americans," Shabiz cursed. "Always showing off."

The machine finally landed and a lone man stepped out. He was small and thin, with a slightly rattish look to him. He was wearing sunglasses, even though the sun was nowhere to be seen.

The flying machine left quickly, ascending through the dark clouds with a corresponding crack of faux thunder.

Now it was just the two of them.

They approached each other slowly; it was not the first time they had met. Moon was connected to just about every known U.S. intelligence agency—and a few that were not known to all but a handful of Pentagon and White House bigwigs. Shabiz first ran into Moon at a UN function in Vienna in 1999. Approaching him with a massive glass of gin in hand, the slight American recited from memory every nuclear materials processing site in Iran—highly classified information—and then simply walked away. It was the CIA's way of telling MOIS that it was privy even to Iran's most sensitive intelligence. The list of sites was in essence a target list.

Now, here they were again. Different site, different time. Different circumstances. With no less than the end of the civilized world hanging in the balance.

They didn't shake hands. They barely nodded to each other. As it turned out, one of the nearby ruins had a stone table. They walked to it and sat down across from each other. Moon pulled out a Ronson lighter and flicked it. It lit immediately. He placed it on the table between them, to give them light. Then he just sat back and waited.

A few uncomfortable moments passed. Finally Shabiz broke the silence. In halting English, he said, "You wanted to talk—so talk."

Now, Moon didn't even pause to take a breath. "In less than forty hours, the Israelis are going to launch an attack against you—most probably a nuclear attack. Every major city, every major military base, every secret processing site, dam, airfield, you name it, will be hit repeatedly. They will leave nothing standing."

He looked around the ancient ruins, then added, "Not even anything like this."

Shabiz was shocked—and furious. "If that happens, our friends in Lebanon will rain hell down on the Jews and—"

Moon gently interrupted him. "And the Shin Bet and Mossad have the name and location of every key member of Hezbollah and have them under twenty-four-hour surveillance, and when they make their move every one of your friends will be cut down by a laser weapon firing from orbit."

Shabiz felt his jaw hit his chest. He didn't have to ask—his expression said it all.

"Yes—we have such a weapon," Moon said. "How do you think we kept finding those al Qaeda captains in Iraq? With drones?"

Shabiz wiped his brow with a handkerchief. He would have given anything at that moment to have it rain.

"We have no idea what is going on," he finally blurted out.

Moon looked back at him quizzically. "Say that again."

"We have no idea who has those suicide planes or how or where they are being launched," Shabiz said. "We know that the people who have been killed in these attacks have been talking to our political enemies. To you and the Jews. But you must believe me, this plot is not afoot anywhere within MOIS or our military. We are as baffled by it as you."

Moon started to argue with him—but suddenly stopped. He was beginning to wonder if Shabiz might be telling the truth. The initial chatter picked up by the CIA right after the suicide attacks indicated confusion within the Iranian power structure. But that didn't mean much—the Iranians would be smart enough to lay down that kind of smoke screen if they were behind the suicide attacks. But it was the way Shabiz looked that was telling Moon something. He appeared scared, tired and confused, the same way anyone on the Western side who was privy to the situation looked. Plus, just the fact that Shabiz agreed to talk to him also told him something.

But still, Moon was not convinced.

"How can you sit there and claim you lost track of 137 jet fighters?" he asked Shabiz harshly. "Knowing how you people operate, I find that impossible to believe."

"The aircraft used in these attacks were taken out of their storage facilities sometime in the last few months," Shabiz revealed. "They were supposedly sold to scrap dealers, people who would take them apart and get rid of them for good. Most of them could barely move, never mind fly, you understand, and they were a burden to us since the day they landed here. Still, we arrested and executed the maintenance officers who allowed this to happen, but when we looked into their backgrounds we could not find anything beyond the fact that they were told it was the desire of the Supreme Leader himself that these planes be taken away in the middle of the night and turned into junk."

"But how do you know that's not the truth?" Moon challenged him. "Maybe your Supreme Leader is indeed behind all this—that he's eliminating these moderate types for talking to Israel, and that it is you who's been left out in the cold."

Shabiz just shook his head urgently. "No—we *know* that's not true, because . . ."

"Because . . . what?"

Shabiz bit his lip so hard it actually started to bleed. "Because we have the Supreme Leader's quarters bugged," he said finally. "His home, his office. His own personal mosque. His mistress's loft. He doesn't know it, but everywhere he goes, we listen in. If he had any conspiracy going with the people who took those accursed planes, we would have heard it. Seen it. *Smelled* it. And he doesn't. Take my word for it, he's just as confused and frightened as we are."

Another awkward silence. Moon was trying not to have his emotions overrule common sense or his street smarts here. He knew the Iranian culture was based on lying—centuries of foreign occupiers had built into the Persian DNA a propensity to lie; in centuries past, telling the truth to their overlords could spell a death sentence.

"I'm sorry," he finally said. "But I find this to be impossible to believe. There is just no way this isn't a plan by someone high up in your government to finally attack the Israelis. You guys have been bragging about it for years, you and your nuclear programs. Now you've come up with some misdirection strategy—and the next thing we all know, Jerusalem is leveled."

He leaned across the ancient stone table and got very close to Shabiz's face.

"But as I said," Moon went on, "your plans are insane. They will accomplish nothing but flattening this country and killing millions of your people. And even though you might get a few shots off at the Israelis—maybe drop a bomb on Jerusalem or Tel Aviv—you know them as well as I do. They won't leave one person, one duck, one insect, alive in this country—and they don't care what kind of ramifications that causes. And right now, it will set off a chain reaction that will go right around the world. Does that sound wise to you?"

But Shabiz was shaking his head all through Moon's lecture.

"No—you *must* believe me," he said, his eyes darting left and right, as if he was searching for the right thing to say. Then he lit up a bit.

He reached into his pocket and pulled out a wallet. From the wallet came a photo of a Persian girl in her twenties. He put the photo on the table in front of Moon.

"This is my daughter," he said.

Moon was slightly taken aback. She was very pretty.

"Are you going to tell me now you want to get her out of the country before the roof falls in?" he asked Shabiz.

The Iranian agent shook his head emphatically. "No," he said. "What I'm going to tell you is that she too is a MOIS agent. And she is currently out of the country on assignment."

"So?" Moon asked him.

"So—her assignment is Israel. Jerusalem. And while we and the Jews have many differences, I believe we all love our children. And there's no way I would have her stay there if we were planning to launch an attack on Jerusalem—or anyplace in Israel."

And that's when Moon finally believed him. There's no way anyone could act or lie that well. Which meant the whole problem had just grown exponentially. If the Iranian government wasn't behind the suicide attacks, then who the hell was?

The two men just stared at each other across the ancient stone table, the Ronson lighter throwing weird shadows all around them.

Finally Shabiz broke the silence. "So—what are we going to do now?"

Moon just shook his head.

Finally he replied: "I have no idea."

CHAPTER 5

GUNN felt Amanda's fingers touching his face.

Not against his cheek or lips, but along his forehead, like she was checking to see if he had a fever. Suddenly he realized it was daylight again—or more accurately, morning.

"What's going on?" he asked her blearily. "Is room service here yet?"

"'What's going on' is we've landed," she told him sadly. "And that means the party's *really* over."

A minute later, the rear ramp of the C-17 dropped down and Gunn stumbled out into the morning sun. He had no idea where he was, only that it was a desert landing strip and already the sun seemed unbearably hot.

He let his eyes adjust to the brightness. He saw their C-17 was just one of a dozen big aircraft parked here. Bing's laser plane was next to the gunship, but beside it was an even larger USAF C-5 Galaxy cargo plane. A grandunclе to the Globemaster, this particular giant was wearing a freakish camouflage scheme that combined bright red and dull gray.

Off to its left were two more cargo planes. They weren't U.S.-made; rather they were Italian Riat G-222s and the soldiers moving around in front of them Gunn recognized as members of the RAO Draghi, the elite of the Italian Special Forces.

Beside them were two Royal Air Force 340A cargo planes with gaggles of SAS operators sitting in the shade under their wings. Next to them were two more 340As, these belonging to the Kommando Spezialkräfte, German Special Forces. Beside the Germans were planes belonging to the Dutch Korps Commandotroepen, the Spanish Operaciones Especiales, the Norwegian Jegerkommandos and the Portuguese CTOE.

Newman walked up behind him; he'd flown over with Bing in the new C-17. "It's like an SOF convention, isn't it?" Newman said.

"Or a Woodstock for operators," Gunn replied. He looked around the airstrip. It was just a runway. No buildings, no control tower. Nothing. "Where the hell are we, anyway?" he asked.

"Israel," Newman replied. "Where else?"

WITHIN a few minutes, the principal officers from each SOF unit were assembled in the back of the big, oddly painted C-5. This plane was serving as the gathering's command aircraft.

The commanding officers sat on the floor of the gigantic cargo hold as a man in civilian clothes and possessing a Texas twang stood on an ammunition box and addressed them. He was never introduced—but then again, he didn't have to be. It was obvious he was CIA.

He had a screen and a projection unit set up, but after many attempts he couldn't get it to work. Finally, he just began the briefing without it.

"The plan is simple," he said, after first making sure everyone could understand English. "But only because we have no other choice but to keep it simple. So here goes: Every unit here will be dispatched to a point in a country bordering Iran: I'm talking about Turkey, Armenia, Azerbaijan and Turkmenistan—they're all on board with this, though on the down-low, of course. Pakistan, Afghanistan and Iraq are already covered by SEALs, Delta Force and U.S. Marine Recon.

"Put it all together and we're going to be surrounding these Iranian bastards. And if we can pinpoint where these suicide planes are coming from, the nearest SOF units will go in and take them out. Those units not assigned to land sites will be put on ships off the coast in the gulf and in the Caspian Sea, ready to do the same thing.

"Now, the Iranians will be very aware that we're doing this—that's the whole point. And if they choose to fight us when one of us goes in, then at least we'll know who the real enemy is. If it gets heavy, then the next stage will be cruise missile strikes. If it continues to be hairy after that, then it's gloves off and we call in air strikes against them, from all sides. Now, if *that* happens, I can't see any way we can hold off the Israelis—and exactly what we are here trying to prevent will in fact happen anyway. But again, there're not many options here—and not enough time to do anything more than hope for the best but prepare for the worst."

An ominous groan went through those assembled. SOF operators hated anything that was not well thought out—intense preparation was in their genes. This plan sounded as though it had been drawn up on the back of a cocktail napkin. And to what end? They start throwing lead at Iran, and Israel attacks. They don't throw lead at Iran—and Israel attacks anyway.

The briefing continued: "Meanwhile, we've got commitments from a number of countries that are sending AWACS planes to the region as we speak. They will set up an aerial picket line up and down the Persian Gulf coast of Iran. The U.S. laser plane will be in the air 24/7; it will be the Big Gun for this operation. If anything is spotted trying to get through, the laser plane will try to shoot it down first—I'm told it can do this even from very far away. If that doesn't work, there will be many jet fighters in the air at all times and they will be sent in to intercept. Plus, we'll have missile boats and other naval units with antiaircraft weapons on hand.

"The idea is to set up a steel curtain between Iran and Israel and keep it there until we can find the ex-Iraqi planes and destroy them on the ground. And we just better hope they are all in one place."

He paused again and let another wave of grumbling go through the assembled. Then he went on:

"Now the problem is, once whoever is launching these ex-Iraqi planes gets wind of what we're doing, they'll likely step up their assault and try to sneak a few through before we are all in place. So the game will *really* be on as soon as we move out of here."

The spook paused for a moment, and then was uncompromisingly blunt: "We know this plan is fucked up and that our chances of success are very low. We don't have any idea where the suicide planes are coming from—and even if we do at some point, if just one gets through and gets anywhere near Israel, it will be curtains for all of us. But again, we have no choice but to play it this way considering the alternative is to do nothing. So let's all just try our best and go down fighting if we have to."

THE SOF commanders started filing out of the big plane a few minutes later, their written assignments and forward locations in hand.

Soon only Newman, Gunn, Amanda and the CIA officer were left inside the big C-5.

It was obvious that the Heavy Metal plane had not been mentioned in the briefing. Finally Gunn asked the spook: "So, where are we going? Back to New Jersey?"

The CIA man's demeanor turned even more somber. "No," he replied. "But you'll probably wish you had."

He snapped on his laptop, banged it a couple times to get it to work and then revealed a screen depicting a map of Iran.

"When I said we don't have any clue where the suicide planes are coming from, I wasn't being entirely accurate," he told them. "It turns out we've got a satellite photo that shows a flash of something out in the middle of nowhere in central Iran. It's some big freaking desert out there, and it's a very unlikely place for an airfield. And maybe this flash is an aircraft taking off, or maybe it's not. Either way, we didn't want the other people invited to this party to know we have this particular sat photo. I can't really talk about it very much. Let's just say it ain't exactly common knowledge how we were able to get it."

He hit a button and the satellite photo in question appeared on the screen. Gunn and Amanda studied the image. There was nothing particularly unique about it, other than it had a greenish tint around the edges. It showed a large patch of desert landscape in the middle of which a small but bright point of light could be seen.

"So?" Gunn asked the CIA man with a shrug.

"So, while everyone else is getting into their hiding spots," the spook continued, "we want you, your crew and that freaky plane of yours to get to this place ASAP and see what this little clue can tell us, if anything. Your plane is supposed to be invisible and you're packing enough firepower to equip a small army. So you got the short straw."

Gunn looked at Amanda, who just shook her head. They both turned to Newman who looked especially glum. "The Moonman just talked to a real live Iranian poo-bah," he said. "And he's convinced that the initial chatter was right, that no one in that regime knows what the hell is going on any more than we do—which means the situation got a whole lot more dangerous just overnight. The only thing this Iranian gave us was a promise that if they find where these planes are coming from, they'll let us know, but they also want to take care of it themselves, internally. Frankly, with life on the planet at stake, I'm a bit uncomfortable with that. So I think what the agency wants you to do here is important.

"But know this," the CIA man added darkly. "You're

going right into the belly of the beast to check out this one and only clue. If the Iranians find you out there, they'll kill you all. They won't see it as cooperation—they'll see it as an invasion. And if they whack you, no one will ever know what happened to you except the scorpions."

CHAPTER 6

Thirty minutes later

Twenty-two miles off the coast of Kuwait City is the island of Ahwah.

Barely five miles long, and little more than sand and high cliffs, it looked across the Persian Gulf at the coast of Iran, not forty miles away.

On its northeastern edge was a cliff known as Al-za-Ash. At almost four hundred feet above sea level, it boasted one of the highest elevations in the entire Persian Gulf region.

Atop Al-za-Ash was a snowball-shaped building, twenty feet high and twice that in diameter. It was pure white and covered with dozens of curved rectangular panels.

To the untrained eye, the building might have looked like an auditorium or an observatory or possibly an ultra-modern mosque. The people of Kuwait had been told that it was a transfer station for satellite phone calls.

In reality, it was an eavesdropping post—a gigantic electronic ear aimed right at Iran.

Al-za-Ash was jointly operated by the United States and Britain. But unknown to the Kuwaiti government, most of what it heard was also shared with Israel.

Twenty-four hours a day, seven days a week, a small army of specialists listened in on just about every communication originating inside the Persian state. Military phone calls, cell phone traffic between government offices, even chitchat among civilians, from Tehran to Shiraz to Bandar Abbas—all of it was picked up at Al-za-Ash, thoroughly analyzed and then sent to corresponding intelligence agencies in the sponsoring countries.

Literally hundreds of ships passed the cliff of Al-za-Ash every day; the Persian Gulf was the busiest waterway in the world, and its main shipping lane was just a half mile offshore from the huge snowball building. Most of the ships sailing by were oil tankers moving the thousands of tons of crude that left the gulf every day. Military ships of many nations also used the waterway, as did fishing boats and even a few cruise ships and personal yachts. For all of them, it was hard to miss the big igloo under the blazing sun. But few of them knew what it was.

Security for the strange building was less obvious. Hidden in the tall trees along the sides of the cliff were two batteries of Hawk antiaircraft missiles. A nondescript stucco building behind the igloo contained an advanced Patriot antimissile system. A joint force of U.S. Army Rangers and British paratroopers were also on hand, but out of sight in a barracks farther down the other side of the cliff.

The Al-za-Ash listening post was an important cog in the West's effort to monitor Iran at all times. Thus, the heavy security surrounding it.

But with the sudden onslaught of suicide planes, the U.S. Navy had dispatched the destroyer USS *Rushton* to a position off Al-za-Ash for added protection, at least until the proposed "Steel Curtain" was in place. The *Rushton* was an Aegis vessel. It was equipped with the most advanced radar and antiaircraft systems ever created for a warship. Its combat center could control air defense for an entire aircraft carrier group. Watching over the big snowball would be a breeze.

It was just ten minutes away from reaching its station when the unidentified blip showed up on Al-za-Ash's radar screen.

THE bogey was up very high, around fifty-five thousand feet, and passing over northern Iran when it first appeared. A quick check of communications at every air base in the north half of Iran confirmed that the blip had not originated from any of them. Its present heading was south by southwest, meaning if it stayed on course, the suspect aircraft would pass almost directly over Al-za-Ash in about five minutes.

The listening post's security forces went into action. This appeared to be an opportunity the U.S. had been waiting for: a chance to shoot down one of the suicide planes. The fact that it might be done before the West's steel curtain was put in place was just pure dumb luck.

The Hawk antiaircraft team scrambled from their bunker and pushed the camouflage netting away from their pair of launchers. At the same time, the unit assigned to the Patriot missile battery charged up their weapon to combat-prevent mode. The Patriot's radars were more powerful than those used by the Hawk, simply because the Patriot was built to shoot down high-flying, incoming ballistic missiles and the Hawk was built to shoot down enemy aircraft. Still, both teams were tracking the blip, and by talking back and forth to each other, they confirmed that it would pass over them now in about four minutes. Its destination after that was unknown, but if it stayed on its present heading it would next pass over parts of Iraq and then Saudi Arabia—and beyond that, Israel.

It was the Hawk's new, advanced fire control computers that were able to get an ID on what kind of aircraft it was. According to the heat signature it was leaving behind, it appeared to be a MiG-23, one at least thirty years old. Both of these things fit the profile of previous suicide attackers.

The Patriot battery got the first real lock on the blip, ranging it out and acquiring it in its targeting system. The Hawk did the same thing just seconds later. Meanwhile, the USS *Rushton*, steaming up madly from the south, had also acquired the bogey. They would have three chances then to knock the unidentified plane out of the sky.

But just about the time that the target was three minutes away from passing over the listening post, people on the ground began wondering if what was happening here was all it appeared to be. Of all the flight paths it could have chosen, the blip seemed intent on flying *directly* over Al-za-Ash—and traveling at an altitude that allowed it to be seen on any number of radars, both on land and at sea.

Just as this was sinking in, the bogey radically changed its profile. Suddenly it wasn't streaking across the sky anymore. Instead it was coming almost straight down, nose first, heading right for the listening post.

"Start fire sequence!" The order was heard in both the Hawk battery and the Patriot controls.

Both weapons locked on to the target as it passed through thirty thousand feet. The plane was traveling extremely fast at this point and spiraling madly. Those outside the listening post could see the head of its contrail corkscrewing down, coming directly at them.

It was never really determined which battery fired first—the Hawk or the Patriot. What *was* certain was that the target was hit somewhere around nine thousand feet, and then again at seventy-five hundred feet. The combined fusillade annihilated the aircraft, leaving little more than a cloud of debris floating downward.

Those manning the Hawk and Patriot batteries broke into triumphant high-fiving and backslapping—but it was horribly premature.

Off in the distance but getting closer, a second suicide airplane was coming across the Persian Gulf—and it too was heading right at the listening station. Though it was flying just above wave top level, it wasn't so low that it couldn't be picked up by the Hawk or the Patriot's powerful radars. Yet inexplicably, neither one detected it.

The bogey *was* picked up in the Aegis command room on the *Rushton.* But by the time the crew sent a message to Al-za-Ash, it was too late.

The suicide plane—another creaky old Russian-built MiG-23—came off the water and slammed into the igloo-shaped building doing nearly Mach 2.5. The structure was obliterated in an instant, as were the Hawk and Patriot missile batteries and everyone inside them.

By the time the *Rushton* reached the scene, there was nothing left of Al-za-Ash but a big, smoking hole in the cliff.

CHAPTER 7

"JUST when does this get 'simple'?" Amanda asked.

It was a good question.

The C-17 Heavy Metal gunship—new code sign: AC-17HM—was the last plane to leave the desert base after the gloomy briefing. Several of the SOF aircraft in front of them had trouble getting off the ground. Neither of the usually reliable Riat G-222s could get their engines started properly. One of the German A-340s had a fuel leak. Even the big C-5 command plane had an electrical problem on roll out. It took a call to the Israeli army, who'd allowed the gathering of SOF groups but had stayed away from the briefing, to fly in a portable generator via helicopter to get the huge airplane charged up and on its way. All of this wasted valuable time and only hastened the deadline imposed by the Israelis for launching their preemptive strike on Iran.

Once airborne, the AC-17 headed west. It was soon over the vast expanse of western Iraq. Here it was scheduled to meet an aerial refueler that would fill its massive fuel tanks for the strange mission that lay ahead.

But the refueler, a near antique KC-135 flying out of Incirlik, Turkey, was late getting to the coordinates, even though it had been made aware that the AC-17 was behind schedule. A communications breakdown was blamed for the delay. This forced the gunship crew to circle for almost an hour, burning up the last of their fuel and coming very close to aborting the mission and looking for someplace to land before they crashed.

The refueling itself went badly once the tanker showed up because an unstable weather front had descended upon the area. Battling high winds and vicious rain, the two planes struggled to climb above the weather before finally hooking up.

Once its fuel tanks were filled, the AC-17 turned east to resume its journey. But not a minute later, its inertial navigation station started going haywire. Amanda theorized a static shock resulting from the refueling hookup had caused the problem. They had to shut down the entire navigation suite and reboot it again. It took three tries to get it back to life, but finally it stayed on.

But then, just seconds after that, they had a glitch in their forward control pressurization unit. Strangely, it wasn't losing power; instead it was running too hot.

"I've been flying for fifteen years," Gunn said, as he shut down the balky unit and started the backup system. "I've never had a pressure unit do that before."

"Neither have I," Amanda had replied. "We must have taken some gremlins aboard in New Jersey."

Putting the big plane in a wide 360-degree turn, they ran a complete diagnostic on all their critical systems, and waited, and waited . . . and waited for everything to check out. It took about three times longer than usual. But finally everything was showing green and they were able to straighten out and head east again.

And only *then* were Gunn and Amanda able to study the written orders given to them by the anonymous CIA briefer before they left, a document that included a brief description of the desert area they were flying to. Now, for the first time, they saw exactly what they were expected to do. And that's when Amanda asked her question—*When does this get simple?*—only to find no one on board had a good answer.

The CIA briefer had used that word in describing the overall "Doomsday Deployment" plan. But that was definitely not the case when it came to the Heavy Metal gunship's mission within a mission: the search for the mysterious flash point caught on the equally mysterious satellite photo.

First of all, because of what was known in the satellite picture-taking business as refraction delay, the CIA didn't know the *exact* location inside the Dasht-e Kavir desert where the flash had been seen. They only knew the general vicinity of the burst of light, which according to the crude map accompanying the gunship's orders was within an area more than ten miles square.

Second, the flash had occurred only once as far as anyone could tell—and wherever the CIA had obtained the one and only satellite photo of it, apparently no more were forthcoming.

This meant the gunship team had to do both an extensive air *and* ground search for the cause of the elusive burst of light—and do so inside a hostile country, over unknown terrain that was so hazardous, parts of it, it turned out, had never even been charted on a map. They would have to do all this very quickly as the doomsday clock was already down past twenty-four hours. By the size of the area they had to cover, this mission would normally take three days or more. The Heavy Metal crew would have to do it somehow in a single night.

CAPTAIN Vogel of the 82nd Airborne and Captain Steve Cardillo of the Marine tank squad had joined Gunn and Amanda on the flight deck of the gunship. They had to discuss strategy for the upcoming mission and do it quickly. At this point, they were less than twenty minutes' flying time from crossing into Iranian airspace.

They agreed their first order of business once they were near the search area should be to get the Marine tanks on the ground. Though where they were going to search was pure desert, it was definitely not hard-packed sand that would be conducive to landing an airplane. According to their orders, large parts of the Dasht-e Kavir were made up of almost steppe-like terrain, except the steppes were made of salt. There were mountains out there too—most of them in the form of regular geological formations. But others, again, were made of salt that had simply built up over thousands of years of the wind blowing it in the same direction.

This was not the best topography for running tanks either, especially since it was also one of the hottest places on Earth. That was another reason the gunship crew would have to get their mission done in the course of one night. Because to be caught out in the Dasht-e Kavir in the daytime, meant facing temperatures of 140 degrees Fahrenheit, not good for humans or machines alike.

They had one lucky break, though—or at least it seemed lucky when they first read about it. Their orders said there was an airstrip out there, close to this overly harsh Iranian desert, and in fact it was an American-built air base. But by reading on further, they quickly learned the "base" was actually little more than a single runway and a few support buildings that had been built during World War II as a refueling stop for military planes transiting from the Pacific war to the European theater and vice versa. The tiny base had been abandoned shortly after the war ended and had lay unmolested for the last sixty-five years. Known simply as K-22, recent CIA satellite photos of the place showed its runway was still intact, or at least enough for the rugged AC-17 to set down on.

The base was located about ten miles from the edge of the Great Salt Desert. This meant it would still be a hike to the search area, but at least K-22 was someplace safe where they could land and unleash the tanks, which was an important factor in what was to come.

The thinking was, if the gunship crew *did* find something out in the Dasht-e Kavir that was connected with the suicide planes, there would probably be no time to call for help. The nearest SOF group would be more than four hundred miles away; and because of targeting concerns and so on, the soonest a cruise missile strike could be called in would be at least two hours after any request for one, probably more. Plus the gunship crew would have to be extremely careful about contacting the outside world about anything, as it was obvious that once they crossed over into Iran, they had to stay off the radio and speak only sparingly on their scramble sat-phones.

So, again, if they found anything, they would most likely have to handle it themselves. This meant they would need the tanks, the paratroopers and all the weapons on the gunship—plus a large measure of pure good luck—if they had any hope of success.

GUNN was behind the controls of the huge gunship now; Amanda was now the copilot.

This came about because their new mission was a change from the way the 201st had deployed in their previous actions. Gunn had always flown the unit's gunship, and Amanda had piloted the aircraft that carried the tanks. But the Doomsday Deployment had changed everything and now the AC-17HM was carrying all three aspects of the unit, and as its commanding officer Gunn automatically became the plane's commander. Plus he had experience in firing a gunship's massive weapons. It was just logical that he be behind the controls.

Having Amanda right beside him was a double-edged sword for him, though. He wanted her close, especially considering what was going on in the world. But on the other hand, they'd probably be facing some kind of combat in this hairy apocalyptic assignment, and because he loved her so much, he felt it was his duty to keep her as far out of harm's way as possible.

But then again, she was a soldier and warrior and a

veteran of combat, and he knew she wouldn't have had it any other way.

So here they were—through duty and fate—flying a mission in the same plane, one that could very well be their last.

THEY crossed over the border from Iraq to Iran at 1600 hours, entering Perşian airspace just north of the area of Dezful. Before shutting off their radios, they heard a report on a secure CIA comm-band about the attack on the Al-za-Ash listening post. With it went any hope that the suicide strikes would abate now that the people responsible knew the whole world was watching. Apparently just the opposite was about to happen. Knocking out Al-za-Ash was akin to cutting off the ears of a man you wanted to kill. Whoever the suicide attackers were, or whoever sent them, they knew exactly what they were doing.

The weather grew even worse once the AC-17 crossed over into Iran, but at least now it could work to the crew's advantage. Again, the gunship's Star Skin was so named because it was originally designed to keep airplanes invisible at night. But the futuristic cloaking technology actually worked in all kinds of atmospheric conditions, most times just as well.

One of those conditions was inclement weather. Just as the millions of sensors embedded in the aircraft's fuselage paint could capture star patterns above the plane and re-create them on the bottom, they could also mimic storm clouds, the darker the better. This it was doing now. Gunn had the Star Skin charged up to full power, and by checking his fuselage integrity screen he could see that unless someone on the ground was looking very close at the sky in the middle of this rainstorm, the AC-17 was in very little danger of being spotted. Add in that its four powerful engines were built of "super-quiet" technology, and that the Star Skin paint was also radar-absorbent, meaning it didn't show up on radar at all, the gunship was able to slip into hostile airspace undetected.

THE old airfield was located on the other side of the Zargo Mountains, at the edge of the Dasht-e Kavir, and only about 150 miles south of Tehran, uncomfortably close.

They were approaching the airfield by 1630 hours. There were massive thunderstorms, high winds and lightning going on everywhere around it, but again, this was a plus for the gunship crew. As soon as Gunn spotted the airstrip through his reverse-infrared goggles—a sort of advanced night-vision technology that worked just as well in the daytime—he switched on the gunship's exceptional ground imaging radar. This was how they got their first real close-up look at the abandoned K-22 airfield.

They'd been told that the only thing waiting for them at K-22 would be scorpions and dust devils, and at first that seemed to be the case. The radar imager gave them a picture of the terrain that was so clear that despite peering through a very heavy cloud cover, it looked like it was being broadcast in HDTV. Studying this image, they saw just the long, cracked runway and a ghost town of small buildings clustered at one end. The runway was all they really needed. This would be a cold landing, of course, with no aircrews waiting to service the big plane, no air traffic people guiding it in. But both Gunn and Amanda had performed dozens of landings like this one before, never with any problems.

Still, once overhead, Gunn circled the base a couple times. He was looking for any obstructions that might be on the runway, but it seemed clear, at least through the radar. He glanced over at Amanda who just shrugged and looked back at him.

"It sure isn't O'Hare," she said. "But I guess it will do."

Gunn eased the big plane down below the thick cloud layer. They broke through at about twelve hundred feet. The runway was just off their nose, right where it was supposed to be.

He lowered the gear and started setting the controls for landing. Again, the AC-17 had retro-rockets on its wings and fuselage that helped it land and take off in extremely short distances. But these extra-added features would not be needed here. The runway was plenty long to handle the big cargo plane.

Gunn continued floating them down, everything on his control panel reading green. It was so routine, his mind wandered a bit, thinking about how they would spend the next hour here. They would unload the tanks and some of the paratroopers, then . . .

That's when Amanda started calling out their descent numbers.

Eight hundred feet . . .

Gunn fingered the throttles, pulling them back gradually as the big plane dropped out of the sky.

Five hundred feet . . .

He confirmed gear and flaps were down. The ground was rushing up at them fast.

Three hundred feet . . .

Flaps locked. Engine thrusters ready to be set at reverse.

One hundred feet . . .

Fifty . . .

Suddenly, a crackling noise. Then a sheet of flame went right across the plane's windshield, followed by a storm of broken glass and then tracer rounds, coming from all directions. There was an explosion and the big plane shuttered from stem to stern and back again. All this happened in a matter of two seconds.

Gunn felt like he'd been hit on the head with a sledgehammer. He was seeing double, and stars were spinning before his eyes. He saw Amanda's hand reach over and push the rocket-assist activation control. Suddenly the big AC-17 was shooting almost straight up in the air.

Only then did Gunn realize he'd been shot.

He looked down at his hands; they were covered in blood. So was the front of his flight suit. Amanda was wrestling with the stick, trying to get control of the big plane as it shot up into the sky. She finally killed the rocket assists at seventy-five hundred feet and leveled out.

Then she turned her attention to Gunn.

"You're OK," she said with such a comforting tone that Gunn believed her. True, something had come through the side window and grazed his cheek. But most of the blood was coming from the dozens of small cuts he'd received on his hands and face from the explosion of glass that followed.

"I'm a multimillionaire for God's sake," he said, brushing the glass shards from his flight suit. "Do I really need this crap?"

Amanda yelled to the people in back: "Everyone OK?"

"Just a bunch of new ventilation holes," was the reply. "But that's it . . ."

She checked the flight controls.

"Primaries are all OK," she reported, scanning the forward panel. "Nothing is leaking. Nothing is getting hot. Everything is green—except . . ."

Gunn spotted it the same time she did. There was a large hole in the ground-imaging radar screen.

"God damn," he cursed. "The one thing we really need, and it's got a bullet in it."

Amanda pushed the diagnostic control panel. Somehow the GIR screen was still working, though the images it was displaying were skewed. But the radar imager itself had been hit, and now it would only work in safe mode, meaning about 80 percent of its capability had been lost.

One of the paratrooper medics was quickly up on the flight deck, patching Gunn's biggest wound just below his left eye and cleaning off his multitude of smaller ones.

The medic showed him several large dents in his crash helmet.

"Good thing you were wearing the bone dome, sir," the medic told Gunn, "or you might have gone home in a box."

Gunn thanked the medic, took a deep breath and collected himself.

"OK, so what the hell happened?" he asked Amanda finally. "Who was shooting at us?"

"No idea," she replied, turning the big plane around, and heading back toward the base. "But I saw tracers going both ways, so maybe we just dropped in on some folks who were already going at it."

Gunn tried to shake the cobwebs out of his head; his skull seemed ready to burst. He needed to concentrate on the problem at hand, but it seemed too freaky. They were supposed to be landing at a deserted air base out in the middle of nowhere. What were the chances that they would come down in the middle of a gun battle?

Amanda activated the plane's landing-assist video playback. A video camera located in the AC-17's nose automatically turned on whenever the front gear came down, giving the pilots the option of landing via video. It was rarely used, though, as most pilots preferred to land their plane via twenty-twenty eyesight. But now, playing back the footage might help them understand what had just happened.

The TV screen on their control panel was filled with static at first. But the playback cleared up just about the time the AC-17 was descending through five hundred feet. The runway could be clearly seen, as well as the two support buildings on their left. Behind the buildings were some shallow hills that gradually climbed up to the side of the small mountain range, which bordered the airfield on its eastern side.

And sure enough, they could see telltale muzzle flashes coming from these hills, as well as from one of the support buildings just as the airplane was about to touch down—indications that would not normally show up on the ground-imaging radar. It was this barrage that had caught Gunn's side of the plane and had caused his still-pounding headache.

But when they checked with the people in back, they discovered the "new ventilation holes" were on the starboard side of the plane, meaning it was the opposite direction of the barrage that caught Gunn. Unless they had blundered into an ambush, which seemed unlikely since the only weapons fired at them were small arms, the only other conclusion was that they had indeed interrupted a gunfight that was already in progress.

But this was a big complication—at a time when they didn't need any further complications. They had no idea who was shooting at who down there—and it was never wise to land in a "hot zone." But Gunn knew he didn't have any alternative. What were they going to do—fly back to Israel?

"Let's get their attention," Gunn finally decided, sending an order back to his gun crew to get ready.

"Again, you mean . . ." Amanda corrected him.

THEY returned to a point above the base and started a rapid descent from the west, opposite from the last time when they'd come in on a north–south heading.

Amanda was right: whoever was fighting down below must have been shocked to see the huge AC-17 come out of nowhere—and then disappear just as quickly. This time, Gunn broke through the cloud cover and then activated his weapons panel. He leveled off at five hundred feet and, seeing tracer fire still going back and forth across the runway, turned his nose toward the nearby mountains and then pushed his weapons panels.

Every weapon on the AC-17 fired at once. The barrage was so massive, it created a shock wave that actually burned away the top layer of rain and fog. The noise was tremendous.

It lasted only two seconds—but that was enough for whoever was below. No sooner had the gunship stopped firing than all tracer fire going across the runway ceased as well.

By reactivating their reverse-infrared goggles, Gunn and Amanda could see the previously hidden figures fleeing wholesale into the hills on one side of the base and just as many more were heading into the desert on the other.

In other words, both sides were in full retreat.

"OK—we got their attention—*again*," Gunn said, finally landing the plane. "Now we've got to find out who they are . . . and quick."

CHAPTER 8

THIS had not been a good day for the Shalam Shabak.

The small, armed group—it consisted of fewer than thirty fighters—usually slept during the day, their homes being the salt caves just inside the western edge of Dasht-e Kavir.

They did their best work at night, scouring the surrounding desert and digging up scrap pieces of war machines that had fought here, many of which had been destroyed, abandoned or shot down over the many years.

From these scraps, the Shalam Shabak, also known as the SSK, were able to fix weapons or make bullets or, sometimes, if the pieces were large enough or still usable, sell them on the black market to some country in desperate need of parts. Countries like Iran.

There was an ironic twist to this, because the SSK, though comprising Iranians, were also anti-Iran. That is, they were enemies of the current regime in Tehran, preferring the equally bad old days of the shah.

For years they had called Iraq their home, but only because Saddam Hussein had tolerated them owing to their anti-Tehran views. Saddam had sporadically given them money and ammunition, if just to needle his archenemies in Tehran. But things changed after the U.S. invasion of Iraq.

With Saddam disposed, the SSK lost its sponsor. The invading Americans continued to tolerate them but gave them no support. The Turks hated them and launched air strikes on them whenever they could. The Kurds too detested them and ambushed them regularly. The Revolutionary Iranians, of course, reviled them, shooting them on sight—unless they had a valuable piece of war materiel to sell.

So the SSK eventually infiltrated back to their homeland and became skells. Feeding themselves on mountain goats and bird eggs, they plotted and prayed and dreamed of the day they would bring down the religious fanatics currently in control of their beloved Persia and return it to a dictatorial monarchy.

But that dream took a hit this afternoon when they were engaged by another band of skells, who also called the Dasht-e Kavir region their home. They were the al Qaeda el-Qabek, or the hated QQB. This group's allegiance to Osama bin Laden reached nearly cultist proportions, even though the infamous mass murderer consistently refused to meet their representatives and basically wanted nothing to do with them, as they were made up primarily of amateurs and terrorist wannabes.

Like the SSK, they'd been shunned by all sides after the Iraq invasion, and they too were driven to relocate here, in this weird, uncharted, extremely hot part of the world. The two sides clashed frequently.

The latest gunfight was sparked when a search party of SSK fighters had recovered a wing from a long-ago shot-down Iraqi warplane and was dragging it back to their camp when the QQB attacked. Digging for scraps of metal in the desert was also the chief source of income for the QQB—or at least it had been. Recently, the QQB had been more concerned about the SSK wandering into their territory than fighting them for scraps of metal.

This latest battle took place at the old airfield, which was located almost dead center between territory claimed by the SSK and that claimed by the QQB. The fight ended only when a new kind of warplane showed up and fired more guns than both armed groups had put together.

The frightening display sent both bands of warriors scurrying back to their hideouts. Which was where the SSK was now.

The thirty fighters had revived their campfire and gathered around it to ward off the cold wind and drizzle.

They were disheartened, more so than usual. They'd lost a prized piece of metal during the firefight with the QQB and had used up a lot of ammunition in the fight too. This meant they'd have to go back out there later tonight to try to recover the missing piece with only a few bullet rounds at their disposal.

It was not a pleasant prospect, so the group was particularly dispirited as night finally fell.

That's when the paratroopers showed up.

IT was strange, because the SSK fighters had no idea that while they sat around their raging fire, twenty-five feet from the front of their home cave, grumbling and cursing about the QQB, they were slowly being surrounded.

One moment the desert fighters were trying their best to stay warm; the next thing they knew, there were huge gun barrels pointing at them from all directions.

Then these gigantic creatures began showing themselves, wearing weird camouflage capes over their uniforms that almost made them dissolve into the background. Their faces were covered, and their helmets were so futuristic-looking they could have been invaders from another planet.

It was pointless for the SSK fighters to go for their guns, empty as they were. Whether these intruders were Iranians or Turks or someone else, they were obviously a much higher level of warrior than the SSK. Which meant the SSK was at their mercy. At the moment, they were sure they were going to be massacred.

So it was a surprise when one of the armed men took off his goggles and his camouflage cape and in doing so revealed a shoulder patch of the American flag.

This man then said, "Whoever the leader here is, come with us. The rest of you guys, sit tight."

* * *

FIVE minutes later, the leader of the SSK was on his knees begging.

"No Abu Ghraib! No waterboard—please!"

They were about a quarter mile from the tiny SSK base. Captain Vogel, commander of the gunship's paratroopers, and ten of his men were surrounding the SSK leader—the rest were back guarding the other SSK fighters. Gunn was also here, as was the paratroopers' medic. By using their high-tech reverse-infrared night-vision goggles, it had taken them barely ten minutes to find the tiny SSK hideout. Now it was important that they question the SSK's leader, but so far all they'd gotten out of him was his name: Ahmed al-Kat.

The medic was trying to give the man water as well as look at a wound he'd suffered during the gunfight earlier at the deserted base. But the guy was just too frightened to cooperate. Even though he understood and spoke some English, he was convinced the Americans were going to torture him.

"No waterboard—please! No Abu Ghraib!"

"This is such bullshit," Gunn said more than once. "*Such bullshit . . .*"

It was still rainy, still cold, and night had fallen. The gunship's unexpected reception at the supposedly deserted airfield had thrown a big monkey wrench into their plans. But just for their own security, they had to know why there was a small war going on in this place that they had to operate in.

The first step, though, was they had to first convince al-Kat that they didn't mean him any harm.

But he just didn't believe them.

It was Vogel who finally came up with an idea. He took out his sidearm—a Glock 9mm—and handed it to the SSK commander.

He said, "If anyone tries to torture you, use this to shoot him—deal?"

The SSK commander was astounded. He took the gun and carefully laid it on the ground next to him.

Then he began to talk.

He told them who he was and who his men were. He explained why they were out here, in the middle of nowhere, fighters without a country. He emphasized that while they might not be friends with America, they weren't exactly enemies either.

However, the people they were fighting when the gunship showed up were definitely someone the Americans should know about.

"They are the QQB," he said. "Al Qaeda—but so bad even bin Laden doesn't want them. They are vicious and they feel unappreciated. If they ever get any real support, it will be they who are flying airplanes into your buildings next."

He explained that both the SSK and the QQB kept their meager groups together by scavenging parts of materiel ruined by the various wars fought in the region over the years.

"But the QQB has changed in the past month or so," he went on.

"How so?" Vogel asked him.

The SSK commander shrugged. "They suddenly have better weapons. And unlimited ammunition. They look better fed. They even have uniforms now, sort of. We haven't seen them picking up scrap very much lately either; it seems all they want to do is keep us away from their territory these days. It's like they suddenly found a treasure in that part of the desert."

Vogel looked at Gunn and said, "Or maybe it was 'the treasure' that found them . . ."

CHAPTER 9

Tel Aviv

The taxi screeched to a halt in front of the nondescript building on Haifa Street.

Colonel Doug Newman checked the address he'd written on his hand and looked out the cab's window. He was in a business district on the northern edge of the Israeli capital. There were a half dozen buildings here that went around an odd, out-of-place cul-de-sac. Each building was twenty stories high and made of dull gray steel. They looked more like hotels than anything else. Each building even had a doorman, or what appeared to be a doorman.

Even though the address said Haifa Street, Newman had heard this place had an unofficial nickname: Gideon's Circle. Where all the spies worked.

Mossad. Shin Bet. Sayeret Matkal. Israeli Air Intelligence, Naval Intelligence, Army Intelligence. They were all right here, or at least their main offices were, along with a few more belonging to the Israeli State Police, the Regional Intelligence Command and, Newman was sure, somewhere, a few rented by the CIA.

That's why the doormen were all carrying Uzis.

In a vacant field about a hundred yards from the circle, there was a Patriot/Arrow antimissile battery set up. A joint U.S. Army–Israeli Defense Force team was manning it. Its generators were making a piercing whine that was bouncing off all the buildings nearby. Farther down the road was a security checkpoint manned by a dozen heavily armed Israeli soldiers. Two Israeli air force Cobra attack helicopters were parked nearby.

Must be the place, Newman thought.

He paid the driver and climbed out of the cab. It was early evening by now; it had taken him much longer than he expected to get from the desert to here. He breathed in the humid air and almost coughed. A long night was about to begin.

He saw three men with rucksacks and suitcases rushing toward him. They were not interested in him—they wanted his cab. Just by looking at them, Newman could tell they were Israeli operatives, probably Mossad agents. It was also obvious they were going somewhere, to do God knows what, and in a great hurry to get there.

Now as Newman looked around the cul-de-sac, he could see several more groups of agents, also with rucksacks and luggage in hand, also trying to locate taxis. It was a good rule of thumb that if you saw a Mossad agent in a hurry to get someplace, things were not so good in the world.

He walked up to the nearest building—333 Haifa Street—and nodded to the doorman. This person was dressed in a muted brown suit and a straw hat that was more readily seen in Brooklyn or at a racetrack. But he subtly moved his jacket to one side to reveal an Uzi stuck in a quick-release holster. Newman flashed his ID, and the doorman allowed him to go in.

The only thing in the lobby was a desk that seemed right out of a Hilton Hotel. Newman again showed his ID, this time to the pretty girl behind the desk. She gave him a room key.

"Twelfth floor," she said sweetly, with a wink. "First door off the elevator. I believe your friend just arrived as well."

A minute later, Newman inserted the door key in a slide lock and entered a large well-lit suite. It looked like a newspaper editorial room—several rows of desks and cubicles, each occupied by someone staring into a computer screen and typing madly. It also seemed just as busy as a newspaper an hour before deadline. But it was also very quiet; everyone in the suite was speaking in hushed, urgent tones.

No one greeted him, no one even looked up when he walked in. He was just beginning to wonder if he was in the right place when he heard a familiar voice behind him.

"Colonel Newman? Over here . . ."

Newman turned to see Lieutenant Moon waving from a glassed-in office located almost directly behind him.

Newman walked into the office, noting it had two desks, two computers, two phones and one large window that looked out on Tel Aviv, and that was about it.

"No coffee machine, Lieutenant?"

Moon just shook his head. "They don't allow drinking or eating anything around their equipment," he said. "I think it's because it's all on lease."

It was only then that Moon stood up and gave Newman a somewhat mechanical salute. They'd known each other for years, but Newman never got over the notion that somehow Moon outranked him.

"Welcome to CIA extension office 212," Moon told him. "Maybe the last piece of office space available in Gideon's Circle. We were lucky to get it."

Just as the SOF units at the desert briefing had been given their assignments, so too had Newman and Moon. In fact, their job was as important as those handed out to the conglomeration of special ops teams—maybe even more so.

For what lay ahead, Newman and Moon were to act as liaisons with the combined Israeli intelligence services, the people who occupied Gideon's Circle. Their job: Make sure the Israelis didn't jump the gun. Make sure they let the U.S. and the other allies try to ID and then end the suicide plane attacks before launching its preemptive strike on Iran, an act that would start the Doomsday dominoes falling and probably unleash a catastrophic nuclear war.

Newman and Moon would be the cutouts through which everything the 201st and the other allied forces were doing in the Persian Gulf would be funneled to the Israelis. Again, it was their job to keep the lid on—until the Israelis decided to launch their strike no matter what.

Newman sat down at the desk next to Moon and contemplated the computer screen in front of him. It was sectioned off into four equal quarters. One bore the logo of the CIA; another, the Joint Chiefs. The third was simply labeled "Local Intell." The fourth was a digital time display. It was ticking down: *twenty-three hours, thirty-six minutes, ten seconds . . .*

"Click on any of the first three boxes and you'll get the latest dope," Moon explained to him.

Newman did so: he clicked on the Joint Chiefs logo and was directed to a web page that was displaying bits of information like a Teletype machine. The latest: Forensic work was being done on the black box from the Kuwait City suicide plane attack, as well as the one just recovered from the aircraft that hit the eavesdropping station at Al-za-Ash. The experts were trying to confirm without a doubt that both were indeed from ex-Iraqi planes, though the results would not be available for seventy-two hours. Newman next clicked on the CIA logo and read that just about every major country on the planet was helping in some way to ease the crisis, either overtly or covertly—all except the Russians, who had been strangely silent.

"Bastards," Newman said under his breath.

He clicked on Local Intell. It was short and sweet. It listed the number of Israeli F-15 fighter bombers that were now waiting on runways at bases all over the country, loaded up with tactical nuclear weapons, ready to launch against Iran.

"Our job," Moon went on, "is to take the info from the first two and provide it to the third—that being the Israelis."

"And those numbers counting down?" Newman asked.

"Strictly CTA," Moon said. "Countdown to Armageddon."

Newman just shook his head. His wife and what was left of his family—his daughter had been killed by terrorists the year before—lived near Las Vegas. The enormous Nellis Air Force Base was nearby and he was sure that if this situation got out of hand and people started throwing around intercontinental ballistic missiles, one of them would be aimed at Nellis and would take out Vegas along with it. What was formerly just all desert would be desert once more.

What a fucked up state of affairs this is, he thought. He had no way to warn his wife, no way to even let her know where he was. They would die in separate locations, with no idea how the other spent the last moments of their lives.

Moon seemed to sense what Newman was thinking—but it was not the lieutenant's way to be all warm and fuzzy. He was a dour, unapologetic pragmatist, and Newman was about to get a large dose of his brand of reality.

"Nothing really matters here—how this thing starts or who starts it," Moon told him starkly. "We can wonder 24/7 as to who could be behind these suicide attacks. Or maybe whether it could be more than just dead-end Iranians causing this craziness. After my trip over there, I'm fairly convinced the Iranian government has no idea who's responsible. But in the end, just who's doing it could be one big moot point."

"Meaning?" Newman asked him.

Moon dropped a document on his desk.

"You should read this," he told Newman. "It really cuts it all right down to the bone."

The document was titled "The Falklands Factor."

Newman leafed through the document; it ran more than fifty pages and was heavy with graphs and addendums. He turned back to the first page and read the introduction and then the conclusions section. He felt his eyes go wide and his jaw drop a little more with each sentence he read.

Basically this was a study done by DARPA and MITRE, two government-sponsored think tanks, that said that in certain times and under certain circumstances, war became inevitable no matter how hard anyone tried to prevent it.

The study stated that "miscommunications, confusion at the top of the military command and political structures, and even glitches in the world's smartest, most sophisticated weaponry could all wind up creating a witch's brew of unpreventable actions just hours prior to a conflict. This perfect storm of mistakes, misinterpreted orders and intangibles will make armed conflict organically impossible to avoid."

As the prime example, the study cited the unlikely conflict known as the Falklands War, hence the report's name. The Falklands are two pinpricks of land off the coast of Argentina. The British had ruled them for years and the few hundred inhabitants of the islands considered themselves British. However, Argentina also laid claim to the islands and not everyone in the international community disagreed with them, including the British themselves. During the 1970s and early '80s, the Argentineans and the British would get together every six months to discuss transferring control of the islands over to the Argentineans, mostly because it cost the U.K. too much to keep the faraway, windswept, practically Antarctic islands within the realm. Even though notes of these meetings were public knowledge, and even though the British and Argentineans clearly realized at some point the Falklands would change hands, inexplicably during these meetings, both sides became convinced the other side was hearing them wrong and that they were prepared to go to war over the islands.

And that's exactly what happened: Despite diplomatic efforts, letters back and forth, pleas from everyone up to and including the pope, the two unlikely combatants went to war over the two unlikely islands. It was almost as if fate had dictated this was something that had to be done.

"But the Brits won that war," Newman said to Moon after reading the conclusions page.

"That doesn't make any difference," Moon replied. "The war started despite huge efforts to prevent it—it was an irreversible cycle. And what the other forty-nine pages of that report says is that this war we are facing today is going to start as well—and no one can stop it and it won't make any difference who 'wins.' It will be fought—and it will bring about the end of the world as we know it.

"It even says 'impossible, or even seemingly otherworldly things' are going to happen, simply because the stars have aligned and it appears the world *is* destined to end. That's why it's marked extreme top secret. Strictly for the scariness aspect."

Newman looked back at him in quiet horror. "So you're saying those people on the streets of New York chanting 'The end is near' *were* right?"

Moon removed his sunglasses—a rarity—and rubbed his tired eyes.

"If you read that report cover to cover like I did," he said wearily, "then there is no other conclusion to make. No matter what we do, no matter how hard we try—or how hard anyone tries—what's coming cannot be stopped. All sides will be unreasonable; people are going to do stupid things. Israel is going to overreact to Iran, and Iran is going to overreact to Israel. And the technology we need to help us stop this thing will fail right when we need it the most. It will happen, *no matter what.* And when it does, this planet won't be anything like it is right now."

But Newman was suddenly furious. Usually a cool customer, all this was finally getting to him. He *wanted* to see his wife again. He *wanted* to see his grandkids. This faddish doom-and-gloom stuff was getting out of hand.

"I refuse to believe any of that mumbo jumbo," he finally told Moon harshly. "There's probably a study like that for every conflict we've fought in the past fifty years. It's just a way to ramp up those assholes in Washington, get them scared so they don't question what's going to be done out in the field. You know how that game is played."

But Moon was shaking his head. "I know, Colonel," he said. "But I actually read this report closely. It makes a lot of points that seem irrefutable."

Newman could feel his face go red. "'Impossible, seemingly otherworldly things are going to happen?'" he said mockingly. "That's fucking nonsense."

Moon just shrugged and adjusted his sunglasses.

"Did you see what happened at Al-za-Ash?" he asked Newman. "It's just one example, and I'm not sure if it was otherworldly or impossible, but it sure was weird that those batteries tracked one suicide plane and completely missed the other."

Newman felt sick to his stomach. He was tired, hungry. Burned out. He needed a drink.

"God damn, do they have booze here?" he asked Moon unexpectedly.

The diminutive lieutenant was thrown by the question. "In this building, you mean?"

"No, I mean in Israel, in general," Newman replied anxiously.

"I believe so," Moon said.

"Then get your hat and purse," Newman said. "We're going to get a drink . . ."

"A drink?" Moon was stunned. "With all that's happening? We just got here . . ."

"We're getting a drink," Newman told him testily. "And that's an order."

THEY walked out of the building into the hot night and turned left, toward a more populated part of the city.

"I've read hundreds of reports like that one," Newman was still grumbling, wishing he had a cigarette even though he'd given up the habit years before. "Just because those eggheads at DARPA and MITRE say it's true, that doesn't automatically make it so."

Moon could barely shrug in reply. "I've read many of the same things over the years too," he said. "And yes, they are not infallible. It's just that when you take everything into consideration, again like what happened out there at Al-za-Ash. And what all those people were screaming about back in New York. The bad economy. Oil out of control. Weird diseases. Mass killings. Maybe these *are* things that lead up to some catastrophic event—and we just can't see them because we're in the middle of it."

Newman pulled Moon to a stop. "Lieutenant, you are hereby ordered not to engage in this kind of conversation again, understand? It won't do the situation or our own constitutions any good."

Moon looked back at him queerly. The strange little man wasn't used to people ordering him around, superior officers or not.

"Certainly, Colonel," he finally said.

They came upon a café. It was nearly empty, as were most of the streets around them. This was not surprising, but it was a bit disconcerting. All eligible young people in Israel, males and females, were either in the regular military or the reserves. The country was in a state of emergency so most of those people were at their bases, ready for war to begin. Anyone else was just too scared to come out of their homes, as they were expecting the Iranians to attack them, somehow, someway, at any moment.

It was dark inside the café, but Newman was thrilled to see that there were liquor bottles behind the bar. He and Moon sat at a table in the darkest corner of the place.

A tired old man appeared and took their order. Newman wanted a triple shot of their strongest liquor. Moon would have a domestic beer.

As they were waiting for their order, a woman appeared at the door of the café and immediately approached them.

She was dressed like a stereotypical gypsy; she was even carrying a small crystal ball.

She stood before their table and asked in broken English: "May I tell you your future?"

Moon began to politely dismiss her, but Newman beat him to the punch.

"Get lost," he told her bluntly.

She was surprised at first by his reaction, but then her dark eyes narrowed, as did the many creases on her face.

"You, my friend," she said darkly, "for you, I don't need a crystal ball to tell your future. Even a deaf goat would know what's about to happen to you."

She stared Newman straight in the eyes and was silent for a few moments. Then she said, "It's true . . ."

"What's true?" he snapped back at her.

"What you just read," she said. "It's all true. Time is running out. The end *is* near. And there's nothing you can do about it . . ."

PART THREE

CHAPTER 10

LIEUTENANT Bada Bing looked out his cockpit window at the dark waters of the Persian Gulf below and thought, *What the hell am I doing here?*

The new C-17ABL was nothing like his former aircraft. When the 201st had its original trio of airplanes flying, Bing had piloted the Jump Ship, the C-17 that carried the unit's company of 82nd Airborne paratroopers. Back then he'd perfected a maneuver where he could get the big C-17 to go into a controlled stall and hover long enough for the hundred or so paratroopers in the back to jump out and land in an area no bigger than a baseball diamond. It took a lot of practice and a lot of drama to pull off the maneuver, but he'd loved doing it and loved putting the paratroopers exactly where they had to go.

Now he was flying an airplane that looked like something out of a low-budget *Star Wars* movie.

His job was to hook up with the swarm of multinational AWACS planes that would make up the Steel Curtain separating Iran from Israel. The plan called for at least twenty-four of these planes, from countries such as the U.K., Greece, Italy, Sweden, India and even Japan, to join a squadron of U.S. E-3 Sentrys in blanketing the skies above Iran with so many overlapping early warning radar tracks, it would be impossible not to pick up any of the suicide planes coming out of the Persian state.

The laser weapons on Bing's plane—known as ABLs, for airborne lasers—could supposedly fire a lethal beam more than a hundred miles away, much farther than an air-to-air missile fired from a fighter jet. If one of the suicide planes was spotted by the flock of AWACS planes, the bogey's coordinates would be flashed to Bing's plane and he and his crew would try to shoot it down.

It sounded simple—but it wasn't. There were problems with the plan from the start.

First off, the lasers being carried on Bing's plane were not designed to shoot down aircraft; rather they were intended to destroy ballistic missiles while they were still in their ascent stage. According to the company reps Bing had on board, there was a big difference between shooting at something that was rising vertically in a relatively slow "boost" mode and shooting at something that would most likely be flying horizontally, at supersonic speed and with the ability to steer out of the way.

Second, the ABLs didn't blast a target out of the sky—rather, they just heated the skin of the object to the point of puncturing it, causing the object to become unstable and to lose its airworthiness. After that, the hope was the laws of aerodynamics would take over and cause the object to either crash or explode. But again, any target the C-17 would be shooting at would be flying fast, would be able to maneuver and probably wouldn't stand still long enough for the ABL to have much of an effect. Add in that the ABLs actually needed two lasers to work—one to acquire the target and measure the distance to it and then a second to, in theory, deliver the fatal blow—*and* that the weather had to be just about perfect to get a good shot in . . . well, the complicating factors tended to grow exponentially.

In other words, a lot of things had to go right in order for the ABL to do its thing. As one of the company reps told Bing, "Even under the best of circumstances, this stuff usually doesn't work."

And there were problems with the Steel Curtain itself.

In such a chillingly desperate time, one would have thought that all the countries that had promised AWACS planes to the effort would have gotten them in the air and on station over the Persian Gulf as quickly as possible. But that wasn't the case. Just about every AWACS plane promised, including those U.S. planes flying down from Germany, was behind schedule taking off, having mechanical problems on the ground or had been delayed by bad weather. All of them.

As a result, at the moment, the hodgepodge effort to erect an invisible barrier between Israel and Iran consisted solely of two French Navy Hawkeye E-2 EW craft, four similar aircraft from the U.S. aircraft carrier *Ronald Reagan* and another four from the U.S. carrier *Abraham Lincoln*.

Ten small planes doing the work of twenty-four much

larger, more powerful ones. In reality, there wasn't very much steel in the curtain.

The French planes were flying off France's most capital ship, the nuclear-powered aircraft carrier *Charles de Gaulle*—and this too was unusual. Because it just happened to be on a goodwill visit to Bahrain at the time the crisis arose, the *De Gaulle* found itself in the vanguard of dozens of ships speeding to the area to add more firepower and AA capability to the antisuicide plane effort. With the U.S. carriers *Lincoln* and *Reagan* already stretched thin covering the middle and lower sections of the gulf, the *De Gaulle* was given the responsibility for the upper reaches of the troubled waterway.

BING'S first stop after leaving the Israeli desert was the King Khalid Air Base in Saudi Arabia.

He found a message waiting for him there, sent directly from the Joints Chiefs of Staff. It contained his operational orders; the nitty-gritty of what he was expected to do.

He was to take on as much fuel as possible at Khalid and then get airborne. He was to start his aerial picket duty up in the northernmost reaches of the Gulf and work his way down. As the two dozen multinational AWACS planes would be arriving sporadically within the next twenty-four hours, the first aircraft helping maintain Bing's long watch would be the EW planes of the *Charles de Gaulle*.

Bing's orders also told him that he could expect to be airborne for as long as forty-eight hours or more, staying aloft via aerial refueling. He was told to take on as much water and sustenance for his crew as possible.

Bing did as ordered. He got fueled and loaded up with as many ready-to-eat meals the ground personnel at the huge Saudi base could give him. He was even able to take aboard a so-called comfort module, which was basically a Porta Potti his crew could use during their long mission. It would be needed because as it stood right now, every airplane to be engaged in the Steel Curtain effort that had capability to be refueled in flight would stay in the air until the crisis had been resolved, or the world had come to an end.

STILL, the stop at Khalid took longer than Bing had planned—little things just kept breaking down along the way—his radio, his landing lights, the air base's main air traffic control radar. By the time he took off from Saudi Arabia, night had fallen on the Persian Gulf.

Bing steered his huge aircraft northeast to his predetermined point off Kuwait, just south of the marshes of Iraq. He then formulated a course, turned the plane southeast and started making his way down the coast of Iran.

For the first third of the journey, he'd be interacting with the French Navy. Then, he would be passed off to the *Lincoln,* which was sailing off Qatar, and then the *Reagan,* which was down near the Strait of Hormuz. And then he was to turn around and fly back up and do it all over again.

Because his C-17 had pumped-up engines, Bing

could hit 550 knots if need be, and easily cruise at 450. At this rate, he knew he could do one entire circuit in less than three hours.

The French aircraft he would be interacting with first were two, American-built Hawkeye E-2C mini-AWACS planes, basically the same aircraft as flown off U.S. aircraft carriers. The *De Gaulle* also had almost its entire contingent of jet aircraft, including its Rafale and Super Etendard fighters, on deck and ready to launch.

As their first transit began, Bing pressed his ten-man flight crew into service. Some were assigned as spotters, watching over the C-17's radar screens, as well as positioning themselves at the plane's windows with reverse-infrared goggles and visually searching the skies to the east. Others would help the ABL company reps man the pair of laser turrets, trying to take a crash course on the quixotic weapons via a huge operating manual that came with each one. Bing was hoping that he could get at least one circuit under his belt without any problems, if just to allow the crew to get acclimated to the new equipment, and their new, very unusual mission.

But not three minutes after he turned the big plane south, his communication suite lit up like a Christmas tree. It was a message from one of the *De Gaulle*'s Hawkeyes.

They'd picked up a bogey.

THE French EW planes were flying down at twenty-five thousand feet; Bing was way up at angels forty-five. One French plane had picked up a blip in Iranian airspace, moving at very high speed and heading west toward the Iranian coastal city of Bushehr. Communications specialists on the *De Gaulle* were monitoring Iran air traffic control channels and heard Iranian controllers frantically asking the bogey to ID itself but to no avail.

The Iranian air force was not known as an interceptor force. Additionally, almost all of its fighter planes were being held on the ground, in prescramble mode, waiting for what the Iranian government viewed as an inevitable attack from Israel.

So if this bogey was another suicide plane—and it was displaying a lot of similar characteristics to previous ones— it was up to the work-in-progress Steel Curtain to stop it.

Within seconds of getting the call from the French Hawkeye, Bing had his own radar suite locked on the unidentified aircraft.

It was flying at thirty thousand feet, heading due west, a flight path that, with minor adjustments, would put it on a direct line to Israel.

The bogey was about 150 miles away from Bing's location and just about the same distance away from the coast of Iran. One of the restrictions in the Steel Curtain was that no Western military plane could take action on an aircraft while it was still in Iranian airspace *unless* the pilot was absolutely certain that the bogey was in fact a suicider—which, of course, was almost impossible to ascertain.

So Bing would have to wait and track the bogey until it was at least closer to the coast. By that time it would be well within firing range of the laser. Or so he hoped.

Bing told his radar people to keep a lock on the plane no matter what. Then he had his communications officer send a flash message to central command in Bahrain, telling them what was happening. *Then* he opened a secure channel to the French Hawkeye and kept it open. Everything was moving so fast he wanted to make sure that he and the French crew were on the same page when it came to positively IDing the bogey and then taking action against it.

The plan was for the ABL on Bing's plane to engage the bogey first, as they would have a better shot over a longer distance. If the laser failed, the French Navy fighters, which were swarming around the *De Gaulle,* would try to shoot it down. If anything went drastically wrong with that, U.S. fighters from the *Abraham Lincoln,* one hundred miles south of the French carrier, would be thrown into the intercept and would presumably pursue the plane until they could destroy it. But by that time, it might already be approaching Israeli airspace.

Bing knew a lot of eyes and ears in Washington would be following what happened next. He was sure the White House was aware of the situation and looking in as well. Despite all the potential glitches, if the Steel Curtain concept worked, then it alone might be enough to deter the suicide planes.

But several tense minutes had to tick by before Bing could even think about taking a shot at the bogey. He continued to monitor its flight path, slowing down slightly so he would be at the best intercept point when the bogey came into optimum range. He'd already told the ABL reps to warm up the laser weapons. They drew so much power on board, the lights around the huge C-17 actually dimmed when their switches were thrown.

Bing kept checking with the French plane, and by

extension, the people on the *De Gaulle* to make sure they still had the bogey locked in.

The French ship was saying the bogey's flight characteristics matched those of a MiG-23—and there were a number of MiG-23s among the ex-Iraqi airplanes. So a lot of the evidence was indicating that this was, in fact, another suicide plane.

With two minutes to go, Bing called one of the ABL company reps up to the flight deck. He still needed a few holes filled in.

"What's the accuracy rate on these laser weapons again?" he asked the rep.

"In theory we can hit a specific spot on a target up to one hundred miles away with about a two-foot margin for error," was the reply. "Of course the closer we are, the better the chances that we'll actually do something. And, you know, the weather has to cooperate."

The weather over the gulf at the moment was partly cloudy, but rainstorms were moving in.

"What about this weather? Is it enough to screw the pooch?"

The company rep just shrugged. "Like I said before, it will be a miracle if this thing works at all."

Bing's radar officer interrupted the conversation.

"The bogey will be out of Iranian airspace in one minute," the man informed Bing. "We'll be able to start the intercept anytime after that."

Bing turned back to the rep. "What should we aim for?"

The rep replied: "Again, it goes back to the original specs. If we wanted to hit a ballistic missile for instance, we'd concentrate on where its fuel tanks were located.

But on a jet fighter—who knows? Missiles have thin metal skins. Jet fighters, I suspect, have sturdier, thicker skins."

"So?" Bing pressed him.

The man just shrugged. "I'd put the pickle on the pilot. If we take him out, we won't have to worry what he does with a wounded airplane. Theoretically anyway . . ."

"Thirty seconds," the radar man said. "Twenty-five . . . twenty . . . wait, hold on . . ."

Bing looked back at him.

"What's wrong?" he asked.

"Damn," the radar man swore. "We got three more bogeys . . ."

Bing stopped a moment and wondered if he heard that right.

"You said *three more*?"

"Affirmative—we are now tracking three additional bogeys," the radar officer said. "And they're all within twenty miles of bogey number one."

"Who are they?" Bing wanted to know. "Where did they come from?"

"They might be Iranian fighters trying to do the same thing we are," the radar officer replied. "There's an Iranian air base at Thirat. It's right on the coast and about eighty miles south of the first bogey's current position. But that's only a guess . . ."

At that moment Bing's headphones came alive with another message.

It was from the French Hawkeye, which had also picked up the sudden appearance of the three additional airplanes. But because they didn't have the precision of the tracking equipment on the C-17ABL, to them, it looked like *four* suicide planes were coming out of Iran.

Bing made his decision quickly. "Tell the French we are attempting to take out the original bogey with the laser," he said, even though it was not yet out of Iranian airspace. "We can sort out everything else after that." Then he yelled to the weapons team, "Lock on and fire the damn thing!"

An instant later, the C-17 shook from the nose to the ass end and back again. The lights and all the flight control panels dimmed significantly. The noise from the lasers' power generator in the back sounded like something from an old horror movie—all crackling and sizzling. The laser being used was in the top turret—so a harsh red glow enveloped the flight deck, almost to the point of illuminating them all.

All this happened in about three seconds.

Not two seconds after that, one of the company reps who'd actually fired the weapon cried, "Son of a bitch—I think we got a hit!"

Bing was astonished. "You mean it actually worked?"

The man hesitated; he was looking at an instrument that resembled a zoom lens on a camera. It measured the laser beam's intensity; an abrupt interruption in the intensity indicated something had been hit. "Yes—we got him—on the wing . . . I think . . ."

Bing punched up his situational screen and turned on his forward-looking long-range night-vision video camera. He was still heading southeast, traveling at 350 knots at forty-five thousand feet. The French EW airplanes were scattered for about twenty miles in front of him down around twenty thousand feet. The Iranian interceptors, or at least what they thought were Iranian air force planes, were off to his left, at about twenty-five thousand feet. The bogey, now supposedly hit by the laser, was still heading west, still at top speed. But it was losing altitude quickly.

Below them all, steaming northward, was the imposing *Charles de Gaulle*. It was launching some more of its fighters now and its deck was crowded with even more warplanes waiting to take off.

Inside thirty seconds, they would all have a visual on the bogey itself.

Bing let the seconds tick by. Finally, the bogey flashed onto the video screen. But incredibly, the suicide plane, though its wing was clearly on fire, was somehow still under control. And now, instead of heading due west, it began making a wide turn to the south. Bing didn't need the video screen now; he could clearly see the damn thing out his side window, lighting up the night skies for miles. The plane was smoking heavily and trailing bits of fire, but it was still under control and flying.

"This is impossible," the ABL company rep said, watching the plane himself. "We were so close, that bastard should have come apart a few seconds after we hit him."

Suddenly Bing's headphones were filled with voices coming from the French EW planes.

They weren't talking to Bing. They were shouting warnings to the *De Gaulle*. That's when Bing realized the suicide plane was turning right for the big French carrier, and it had the other jets, now clearly seen as Iranian interceptors, right on its tail.

"*God damn* . . ." several people cried at once.

"He'll never make it," the ABL rep said, as they watched the wounded aircraft steer toward the French ship. His voice sounded filled with uncertainty though.

"Can we hit him again?" Bing yelled to him, as the wounded airplane passed down through fifteen thousand feet. It was only about ten miles off the C-17's nose at this point.

"Not unless we risk hitting those French fighters," was the reply.

But it was already too late for another laser shot, as the French fighters, in an effort to protect their mother ship, were rising toward the wounded fighter. The two lead Rafales opened up on the bogey. But at the same time the three Iranian interceptors—ironically they were U.S.-made F-14 Tomcats—fired too. The problem was, many of their cannon shells went streaking by the bogey and right into the French warplanes. In an instant, the French fighters turned away from the bogey and started firing at the Iranians.

"This is insane . . ." Bing cried. "What the hell are they doing?"

The impossible tangle of fighters didn't last long. It broke up seconds later with the Iranians turning tail and racing back to their own airspace. But the distraction had been long enough to allow the bogey to streak past the first line of Rafales. Now Bing could see long tracer streaks and a swarm of air-to-air missiles being fired at the bogey by the second wave of French planes. The missiles were exploding close by and the tracer rounds were hitting the bogey—yet it kept on going.

What came next was thirty seconds of the most astounding flying Bing had ever seen. The suicide plane was twisting and turning its way through the rest of the French fighters. It was too close in now for the French air-to-air missiles to be of any use, but the suicide plane was still taking major hits from their cannons.

"This is fucking *impossible*," Bing cursed—and everyone looking on had to agree. The suicide plane had been hit by a laser, had flown through a number of near-miss missile explosions, and was being raked by cannon fire. Yet, somehow the burning, twisting plane had survived the gauntlet and was now heading straight for the *De Gaulle*.

The crew of the big ship started firing their antiaircraft guns. One of the carrier's escorting destroyers launched a barrage of AA missiles as well. All of them missed. Another barrage was fired, almost at point blank range. But all of it missed too.

The *De Gaulle* opened up with its CIWS Phoenix gun; in theory *nothing* could make it through such a wall of lead. Yet, incredibly, the suicide plane did just that. It smashed into the *De Gaulle*'s superstructure an instant later, causing a tremendous explosion on impact.

The entire crew of the C-17 was stunned. But what happened next was even more shocking.

Even as explosions were racking the big ship, the *De Gaulle* launched six more airplanes, including four bombed-up Super Entenards. These fighter-bombers formed up with the six Rafales already in the air. As Bing put the C-17 in a circle above, the French force flew without hesitation about five miles up the coast and brazenly began bombing the Iranian naval base at Qurum.

The French faced no defensive fire from the base.

No Iranian planes tried to stop them, no AA weapons were fired at them. For the next five minutes, the French went about the business of obliterating the Iranian naval facility.

Throughout the attack, Bing was screaming into his microphone at the French EW planes, telling them to have the *De Gaulle* call off the attackers, but the EW planes never even acknowledged his radio call.

Once the attack was over, the French planes returned to their burning ship and landed on it, even as its crew was still fighting the fires raging all over its superstructure.

Bing couldn't believe what had just happened. No one could.

"What the hell is going on here?" he said aloud. "This is madness!"

That's when the ABL company rep asked him: "Ever hear of 'The Falklands Factor'?"

CHAPTER 11

In the Dasht-e Kavir

Ahmed al-Kat, commander of the SSK, was holding on for dear life.

He was on the back of an American tank, squeezed between two U.S. soldiers, his rifle in hand looking puny next to their huge weapons, and enduring a frightening high-speed ride across the rough terrain of the Dasht-e Kavir.

"Allah Aq-med!" he kept saying, over and over. Loosely translated: "God forgive me!"

The last hour was unlike anything he'd ever experienced. In his talk with the Americans, he'd explained that in addition to being immoral and treacherous, their hated rivals, the QQB, were like ghosts. Even after many clashes with them, and some pursuits, al-Kat and his men had never found the QQB's hideout. They had no idea where their enemy went after they broke off engagements with them. Years of scouring the desert for war salvage and scraps of metal had made the QQBs experts in how to exist in such a harsh environment. They knew how to hide, and they knew how to do it well.

However, al-Kat and his men knew the QQB always retreated back toward the center of the Dasht-e Kavir after one of their gun battles and generally speaking, the SSK knew its way around the hellish salt desert. So, they'd made a deal with the Americans.

The Americans would only say that they suspected the QQB of helping unknown persons within Iran provoke a war with Israel. Even the SSK knew how disastrous that would be for their homeland. So the SSK would help the Americans find the QQB base, and in return the Americans would turn over to the SSK any captured equipment they could liberate in the ensuing fight.

Al-Kat knew this was a very unusual alliance. As a Muslim warrior he was naturally anti-American, anti-Christian, anti-Crusader. But the Americans were here because they had a dispute with the QQB, and the QQB was SSK's biggest enemy. The old saw was that "my enemy's enemy is my friend." So this was a marriage of convenience between his men and the Americans. Just how long it would last was anyone's guess.

Once the deal was made—it included the Americans providing SSK with twenty boxes of prepackaged food, which they called MREs—al-Kat selected five of his best men to join the search party and joined the Americans.

That's when they saw the huge airplane up close for the first time. It was sitting on the cracked runway at the old air base, looking menacing and magnificent at the same time. All al-Kat could think of while looking at it was how much money it would be worth to him if he could cut the big airplane into little pieces.

The Americans had rolled two tanks out of the back of the airplane. Al-Kat knew they were M1-A1s; as a scavenger of military equipment, he was quite familiar with the state-of-the-art American tank. He'd never seen one up close that wasn't in some state of disrepair, though. Usually they were in pieces, after meeting their end via an antitank round, or an extra-large IED or mine.

He and his men were placed aboard the two American tanks for the night's foray, three on each. That's when they saw the huge airplane take off in such a way it seemed like it was a vision from a dream. The plane did not roll a long way down the runway as al-Kat had seen other planes get airborne. Rather, it had great rockets attached to its wings and when these were lit, they lifted it into the sky like the wings of some monstrous fiery bird.

But this was not the strangest thing he and his men saw—that happened just seconds after the big plane was airborne. For one moment, it was huge and filling the sky with its presence.

Then in the next second, it was suddenly gone. Vanished—in the blink of an eye. And all al-Kat could see after that was the stars.

That's when he knew the Americans were not only devils, but they were magicians as well.

Now, to actually be riding on the back of an American tank, going at such high speed, would have been unthinkable when al-Kat woke up that morning. But this was not the only thing that was turning his world upside down. It was the American soldier on his right, hanging on just as tightly as he, as the two tanks moved so quickly over the dark, impossibly rough terrain.

This soldier was not like any soldier al-Kat had ever met—American or not. First of all, the soldier was a woman. A beautiful woman. In fact, she was the most beautiful woman al-Kat had ever seen. She was blonde, had a perfect Western face, huge blue eyes, and a stunning smile. She was prettier than any movie star he could remember.

But she was pressed up against him so tight, he felt as if he was a blasphemer, that he was unclean in the eyes of Allah, to be so close to her, a female who was not his wife or a relative of his wife. Yet, hard-bitten Muslim warrior that he was, another piece of his brain was telling him that it was wrong to think that being so close to such a beautiful creature was not God's way.

So his mind was split. Half of him felt defiled. The other half felt like he had already died and gone on to paradise.

That dying side was a distinct possibility—which was another problem al-Kat was facing. Again, the tank was moving very quickly—sometimes going airborne as it went over some particularly high crest or sand dune. That was scary enough. But it also seemed to be moving with impossible recklessness. Al-Kat and his men had trod this rough ground for years. It was covered with numerous washes, sinkholes, narrow canyons, dried riverbeds and millions of rocks of all shapes and sizes. Yet the monstrous tank was navigating its way through all these obstacles with unearthly speed. And right on its tail was the second tank, holding more American soldiers and three more of his men, and they too were frightened, because every time their tank made a violent maneuver, which was just about every few seconds, he could hear them yelp as he was: *"Allah Aq-med! Allah Aq-med!"*

As frightening and confusing as it was, Commander al-Kat felt that the tank's driver was somehow getting help from above—and in a way, he was right. Because although their huge airplane had vanished somehow—and that had been a scary sight to see—al-Kat had the feeling that on disappearing, it hadn't gone back to where it came from. He believed it was still up there, somewhere. Guiding them through these badlands, making sure they did not crash, did not run into a rock, or drive off a cliff.

He thought this because the beautiful woman squeezed in beside him was talking into a cell phone and whenever she had a chance she seemed to be looking skyward and talking to someone up there, somewhere.

And whenever *he* had the gumption, al-Kat would release his grip on the tank turret's safety handle just a bit and look up ahead, and he was sure that he could see a very faint light coming out of the starry sky leading the tank around all obstacles, as if the pale green beam was telling them which way to go, at high speed, without killing everyone on board. It was weird and mystical, even if he was imagining it.

As all this was going on, occasionally, the beautiful woman soldier would yell to him, "Does any of this look familiar to you?"

He didn't want to tell her that it was hard to see with his eyes shut so tight, so he would just nod or shrug, or sometimes indicate yes.

But whatever he did, whenever he talked to her, his heart felt like it was going to come right out of his chest.

FINALLY, after a very long, terrifying ride, the two tanks came to a screeching halt.

Al-Kat praised Allah that he was no longer moving and promised the Almighty that if he ever got off the tank he would never do anything but walk on his own two feet again.

The people in charge of his tank popped out of the hatch and yelled something down to the beautiful woman soldier.

At the same moment, al-Kat thought he saw a weird ripple go across the sky, right over his head, wrinkling the canopy of stars shining down on him.

The woman soldier leaned over to him, very close, and said, "They have found something in the sand. Can you look at it?"

The next thing he knew, al-Kat and his men were inspecting a series of footprints in the hard sand by the edge of a salt hill. It appeared a group of people was walking eastward, but the wind had covered up most of the tracks.

"This is them," said al-Kat, not 100 percent certain, but at the moment wanting nothing more than to please the Americans. "But there is a chance that they are still far away. They can travel far quickly out here."

The beautiful soldier received another message from heaven. She repeated it as it came in. "Twenty-five meters west . . . near a column of salt."

Two of the other American soldiers disappeared into the night as the two tanks and everyone else waited. They returned in a short time holding something shiny.

They showed it to the woman soldier and the men who were driving the tanks. It was an empty medication vile, not rusty or cracked or pitted by the sands. It looked recently used. Its label read, "Sympathomimetic monoamine epinephrine."

"Adrenalin?" several of the American soldiers asked at once.

Al-Kat heard this and exclaimed, "It is definitely them. Our common enemies are also drug addicts. They become strong from a needle . . ."

There was a brief discussion, including more talking into the cell phones as almost all the Americans unconsciously looked skyward. Al-Kat saw more ripples pass across the starry sky, but the only other sound was the wind. It was eventually decided that they were on the right track, but if the people they were pursuing were taking Adrenalin, that indicated they still had a long way to go. And so did the search party.

They climbed back onto the tank and started out again, albeit this time a little slower.

Somehow al-Kat worked up the courage to ask the beautiful female soldier a question. "Are you an angel?" he said to her.

She was taken aback—he could tell by her expression. He immediately regretted saying anything to her.

But then she smiled and said, "Why do you ask that?"

Al-Kat replied, "For one thing, God himself is pointing out the little things on the ground to you."

She laughed and actually touched his arm. "That's

just technology," she told him. "Electronics and computers."

"But you can also become invisible," he said, pointing to the cloak that was rolled up and hanging from her belt. "You and your friends."

She smiled again. "Electromagnetism," she said. "When I put this on, whatever is in back of me shows up in front. That makes it like I'm not there at all."

This conversation was taking place in between the bangs and bumps of the rough ride on the back of the tank. It was strange though, because no matter what was happening around him, al-Kat could see only her face and hear only her voice.

"But you also *look* like an angel," he told her.

She smiled—and then touched him on his forehead. "You need eyeglasses," she said, laughing.

Al-Kat felt frozen. He shook himself out of it as they hit a particularly large bump, tossing the soldiers on the back of the tank in all directions.

When they settled down again, al-Kat found himself sitting even closer to her.

I am a warrior of God, he thought to himself. *And I will protect all of his angels.*

CHAPTER 12

Tel Aviv

Newman was sitting at his desk inside 333 Haifa Street staring out on Gideon's Circle and the darkened Israeli capital beyond.

The air raid sirens began wailing again, but Newman hardly moved—and neither did any of the other analysts and spooks in the huge suite. The sirens had started moaning around 8 P.M. and had hardly stopped since. The first time there was near panic in the streets—those few people out, running madly down the main thoroughfares, scrambling into bomb shelters, while the Patriot Arrow missile battery in the field near Gideon's Circle lit up, a sudden hive of activity.

But there had been more than a dozen such incidents now and they'd all been false alarms. Besides, Newman and Moon knew that if the spooks in the other room didn't react when the sirens went off, then neither should they. The people in this building knew just about everything that could be known about the current crisis. If an Iranian missile or a suicide plane or a Russian ICBM were heading this way, they wouldn't stick around. Even the people manning the Patriot Arrow battery weren't moving with any real concern.

Still, Newman was tense—and not just because there were now more rumors swirling around that the suiciders had in their possession tactical nukes left over from the Cold War. Or that the French had attacked and destroyed three more Iranian naval bases.

No, he'd expected to hear as much. Rather, the two things running around his head were "The Falklands Factor" report and what the fortune-teller told him. That the world was at a strange confluence of subtle but unavoidable military confusion and overreliance on computer-think, which equaled the perfect storm of a massive and unavoidable catastrophe, was one thing. But how could the fortune-teller be so right on the money? He shuddered a little every time he thought about it.

It was not lost on him either that they were presently at ground zero in the place the Bible said would be the site of the Final Battle. He'd never been a religious man. But he had to admit there were a lot of strange coincidences flying around lately.

Moon was a lot calmer than he; no surprise, the junior officer rarely displayed emotion or anything other than ice water running in his veins. He was doing what they were here to do—passing a steady stream of information from the Pentagon and CIA to the Israeli government, quickly vetting it, but letting 99 percent of it go through. Their job here was to keep the whole of Israel's intelligence community informed and to demonstrate how open the U.S. would be with them with all its intelligence, if only to keep Israel from lighting off Armageddon. Anything and everything Moon was reading from the two websites, he simply cut it and pasted it on the third website for all of the Israeli analysts to see.

Meanwhile, the clock in the lower right quarter of his screen kept ticking down . . .

In the midst of all this, Moon clicked on an alternate site that displayed the headline in a British newspaper. It read in bold type: **SUICIDE PLANES CAME FROM SADDAM'S IRAQ.**

"Damn," Moon swore under his breath. "How did this get out?"

The story detailed what a lot of people had already theorized: that the airplanes being used in the mysterious suicide attacks were the remnants of the pre–Gulf War Iraqi air force, the 137 planes that fled to Iran rather than be obliterated by the U.S. and Coalition forces. Moon briefly summarized the story for Newman, drawing his attention away from the window.

"I thought that was top secret," Newman groaned.

Moon replied, "Not anymore."

Newman finally tore himself from the surreal, gloomy scene outside and walked over to Moon's desk.

He read the last few paragraphs of the British story. They listed the airplanes that the Iraqis had flown into Iran those fateful days back in 1991 and gave a bit of background on each individual model. The writer indicated that he'd received the information from someone close to the situation who could not be quoted directly.

Newman was surprised at the accuracy of the story.

It had the correct number of aircraft that had defected and indicated that seven had been subsequently lost in accidents by the Iranians until they finally decided not to fly them and put them away, essentially to rot.

The writer also expressed surprise that the planes—now exiled nearly twenty years without adequate spare parts or maintenance—could still fly, which also baffled intelligence services around the world. And that's how the story ended.

Newman started to hit the delete button—but then stopped. Something he'd read had just rung a bell.

"Do we have a list of the types of planes that have already gone on suicide missions?" he asked Moon.

Moon hit a few buttons on his keyboard and they were quickly looking at a CIA top secret document that contained field reports from each of the sites where the suicide planes had struck.

There'd been eight in all so far: the first wave of five that had killed the Western-leaning Iranian politicians. The two destroyed in the attack on Al-za-Ash and the one that had smashed into the *De Gaulle*.

On that list, there had been three MiG-23s, two MiG-21s, a MiG-29 and two Su-25s.

"All Russian-built aircraft," Newman said, reading over the list.

"The majority of the ex-Iraqi aircraft were Russian designs," Moon responded.

"I know," Newman said. "But is it strange that none of the French-designed planes from that batch have been used?"

"Not yet, you mean," Moon replied.

"Right—but still think about it for a moment," Newman said, looking over the list again. "If they are sending these planes randomly on these missions, why none of the French planes? You've got almost two dozen Dassault Mirages—great airplanes. If the idea is to mislead or get under, over or around air defenses, those planes are as good as those old Russian shit boxes. Better actually. So why aren't they using them? It isn't like whoever is doing this has to care about insulting the French. That ship has sailed."

"Maybe they're saving them for the big attack," Moon theorized. "Maybe the Russian planes are just fodder. It's a strange question, because if you read the provenance specs on these planes over the past twenty years, *none* of them should be flying, Russian *or* French. Just like that newspaper article said."

Newman pulled his chin in thought and realized he needed a shave. "Yes, maybe," he said. "But maybe not."

They were interrupted by a knock on the door.

It swung open before they could react and they found two enormous "doormen" standing there with a relatively small-stature Asian man.

"Deputy Ambassador Chin Li to see you," one of the doormen said.

Newman dismissed the doormen and signaled for the Asian man to come in. He was middle-aged with graying hair, and he wore an expensive Brook Brothers suit, a silk tie and designer eyewear.

PRC, both Newman and Moon thought immediately.

Chin did a rote bow. He was carrying a large manila envelope. He looked if not nervous, then at least uncomfortable.

He pulled out an ID badge that identified him as a member of the Chinese embassy staff.

"Greetings to you," he said, in near perfect English. "Thank you for taking a moment to see me in these confusing and dangerous times."

"Did you bring coffee?" Newman asked him in jest.

Chin was thrown but for only a moment. He said, "Have you heard the news about Paris?"

Newman and Moon looked at each other and shrugged.

"Tell us," Moon said.

"There's been a wave of bombings," Chin said. "Very large IEDs. Car bombs. Entire buildings blown up. They have poisoned the water supply and have destroyed the power stations. All the bridges leading into the city have been blown up. The city is isolated, is in the dark and is in great peril. This is the work of Hezbollah, of course. Such has been the Iranian surrogate retaliation for what the French have done after the attack on their carrier."

Newman and Moon were astounded. Newman checked his computer and only now did the CIA page say, "Trouble reported in Paris. More later."

Chin said, "But I am not here to talk about Paris or Hezbollah."

He handed the envelope to Moon. "My superiors asked that I give these to you," Chin said. "We are hoping they will help us all in this situation."

Moon opened the envelope to find dozens of images—satellite photographs—taken of the Persian Gulf regions as well as large swaths of southwest Asia.

"These are less than eighteen hours old," Chin explained. "You might be most interested in the photos that depict Turkmenistan."

Moon and Newman studied the photos. Someone had marked several of them with white ink pointing out what looked to be many aircraft flying in formation close to Turkmenistan's border with Iran.

"Those are Russian military planes," Chin told them. "They've been quite active in the past few days, flying back and forth, skirting the border. They seem to be flying when they know your satellites are not passing over the area. But they don't know the movements of our own reconnaissance satellites or those of close allies. In any case, we found this activity unusual and thought you might want to follow up on it."

Newman and Moon couldn't disagree with him. This *was* highly unusual. Why would Russian military planes be engaged in such a show of force when events in the region were just one step away from an all-out devastating war? Every other country in the region, save for those directly engaged in trying to stop the suicide planes, had ordered their militaries to stand down, just to prevent accidents that, according to "The Falklands Factor" report, seem to happen with great frequency in times like this.

And the fact that the Russians were doing this, with planes similar to those being used in the suicide attacks, and in those small windows of opportunity when they knew the U.S. would not be looking in, certainly raised questions about their motives.

"But what does it mean exactly?" Newman asked.

Chin just shrugged. "We don't know," he replied. "We

find it as odd as you do. But again, we felt that we should let you know and we hope you'll pass these on up the line to your superiors."

Ho bowed again and started to leave, but Newman stopped him.

"We thank you, sir," he said. "But I must ask why. Why are you giving us this very valuable if puzzling piece of intelligence?"

Chin's eyes watered up a little, or at least it appeared that they did.

He hesitated, then responded, "Because, my friends, we are just as scared as you."

With that, he turned and left.

Newman and Moon just looked at each other without saying a word until they knew Chin was gone.

Then Moon said, "You know things are really bad when *those* guys want to be helpful."

CHAPTER 13

Inside the Dasht-e Kavir

It was getting brutally hot inside the tank.

Captain Steve Cardillo, commanding officer of the 201st's Marine armor, pulled off his helmet and tried to wipe the sweat from his clean-shaven head, but it was hard to do. Rolling so fast over the terrain of Dasht-e Kavir was one of the most violent things Cardillo and his tank crews had ever done. He was being thrown around so much that it felt like he was on some out-of-control amusement park ride. Still, it was the heat that was getting to him.

"Dead of night and it's this hot?" he said to himself, bouncing around. "Just how close to hell are we?"

It was just past midnight—and just seven hours before the Israeli deadline expired. The gunship's ground team had been at it for more than three hours now. Traveling at high speed, over terrain that was worse than any obstacle course they'd faced at tank school, the handful of paratroopers, the six SSK fighters and Amanda hanging on tight as they tried to track down a bunch of desert dwellers that were so good at hiding, the people who knew them best, their enemies, referred to them as ghosts.

He jammed his helmet back on and tried bracing himself in the open hatchway again. With each passing second, they were getting deeper into the weirdest place he'd ever seen. In many areas, the Dasht-e Kavir was more like a frozen ocean of salt. Frozen, *then* baked. Salt hills, salt gullies, salt wadis, even the salt mountains. Then there were the salt flats, but they were almost as bumpy as the gullies and looked oddly like dried-up rice paddies. And in between all this, vast swathes of quicksand. And above it all, every few seconds, massive bursts of heat lightning.

Cardillo didn't think *desert* was the right word for this place, at least not the section they were in. None of it was flat and hard like one might run into in the American Southwest. Nor was it entirely windblown dunes and soft sand like parts of the Sahara.

Marsh was a better term for it. One that seemed to have been caught in a freeze frame of dull and dirty white. Something that gave off a strange glow at night. Something that looked more at home on another planet.

So the terrain was a big problem, and it was one reason the tanks were running low on gas faster than Cardillo would have thought. They'd also gotten a later start owing to the delay in landing at the old base because of interrupting the gunfight between the two rival desert groups. This meant they had to go faster, and faster meant more gas and the M1s used a lot of gas, even though the 201st's tanks were stripped of everything but weapons, radios and the big turbine engine. Added all together, they were losing time and not covering as much territory as they had hoped.

Now they were approaching their bingo point—and that was making Cardillo worry. A bingo point was a time line. It was the limit that the tanks could go and still have enough fuel to get back to the K-22 air base. Because one thing was for sure: After seeing what was out here, terrain-wise, there was no place that C-17 could set down to retrieve the ground team anywhere but K-22.

The AC-17 too had concerns fuel-wise. Although the gunship had huge fuel tanks, plus the ability to shut down two of its engines to save fuel, it had to conserve enough gas to escort the tanks on the return trip, pick them up at K-22 and then fly them all out to friendly territory. So when the ground team reached its bingo point, there would be no other option. They would have to turn around and go back to the old air base and leave, mission accomplished or not.

All this led Cardillo to contemplate what more than a few on the mission were beginning to think: Was this just a fool's errand that the CIA had sent them on? Poorly planned, misconceived, grabbing at straws?

It wouldn't be the first time.

As one of his crewmen had said, "Is the world *really* being brought to its knees by a bunch of Iranian scrap dealers?"

Cardillo checked his watch again. They were now just two minutes away from the bingo point. This meant that he and Amanda down here and Gunn and Vogel up in the gunship would have to talk about the tough decision to turn back.

That's when his cell phone started buzzing. It was a message coming down from on high.

It was Gunn.

"We just spotted something," he told Cardillo.

"It's not a gas station, is it?"

"Actually, you're not too far off," Gunn replied. "It's in the middle of some quicksand. The wind is skewing the GIR, which is already effed-up. But it's in the same neighborhood as the flash that appears on our spook's mysterious satellite photo."

He gave Cardillo the coordinates and suggested that he send a party out to check the object.

"Just tell them to be very careful," Gunn added. "I don't think many things come back after stepping in that quicksand."

CARDILLO passed the word back to the second tank, and both M1s came to a halt.

They were in a salt gully, heading east, with a small mountain in front of them. The bog containing the mystery object was on the other side. Three of the paratroopers volunteered to go check it out. They donned their Mag-cloaks and, as advertised, disappeared into the shadows of the desert night. Amanda climbed up to the turret. "Be a hell of a thing—a secret air base in the middle of some quicksand," she said to Cardillo.

Cardillo passed her his canteen. "The more I think of

it," he said, "the more I wonder just how many things out here could cause a flash that would be picked up on one—*just* one—sat photo. I mean, it's so damn hot out here, maybe it was just a large burst of heat lightning."

"Could be," Amanda answered. "It's a flash on a sat photo that they won't even tell us where they got it. The agency has never been known for being fast on its feet. But now when we need them, they got us chasing bubbles in the wind."

Cardillo's phone beeped to life.

It was the search party. "We might have found what caused the flash," was the first report.

Cardillo was shocked. "You're kidding, right?"

"Just a guess," the man reported. "But we suggest you drive around and see for yourself."

THE two tanks rumbled their way around the small mountain to see the vast quicksand bog in front of them with an ancient path running along one side.

The three paratroopers had removed their Mag-cloaks and were waving to the pair of M1s.

Once they'd gotten Cardillo's attention, they began pointing to something in the middle of the bog. It was a large object, partially submerged. Both Cardillo and Amanda flipped down their reverse-infrared goggles and zoomed in on the object. Finally, it came into focus.

"You've got to be kidding me," Cardillo said.

"Can you say 'wild-goose chase'?" Amanda asked.

What they were looking at was an old, dirty, rusty, partially disassembled tanker truck.

It was lying on an angle, wheels up, about 250 feet into the quicksand patch. It was obvious that it had been on fire at some point.

"How long do you think that's been out there?" Cardillo asked Amanda.

She really couldn't tell. "I want to say it's been out there since they built that base we landed at," she said. "But the way things are out here—it could have fallen in there a week ago."

Gunn was back on the phone. He was circling the truck now. The wind had died down and the AC-17 was finally getting a good read on it.

"Is that high test or unleaded?" Gunn asked, zooming in on the wreck.

"Either way it was on fire at some point," Amanda told him. "Could that have caused the 'flash' on the CIA's big-deal photo?"

"No way to know," Gunn replied. "But the question is, what the hell is it doing way out here?"

They were silent for a long time. Again, the truck looked ancient—but everything out here did. But *how* did it get out here? There might have been a road here at some point, but with the raging winds able to cover everything in a matter of minutes, it was hard to say if it was just this path or a superhighway.

That's when al-Kat asked to join them on the turret.

"It is them," he said, after looking at the truck through Amanda's goggles. "The QQB. You can see that they have taken pieces of metal off it. They are eating it, piece by piece. Knowing them, they could have pushed it out here by hand. They're known to do stupid things like that."

"Or . . . ," they heard Gunn say over the cell phone.

"Or what?" Amanda asked him.

"Or maybe that truck was out here putting gas in the suicide planes," he said.

They were stumped. There seemed to be no good answer to anything.

It was Cardillo who finally said: "Well, it's all moot now because we are officially at our bingo point. We *can't* go on from here. We did our best, under the circumstances. We found evidence of these QQB guys—but we know they're good at hiding and they don't mind walking long distances out here. We found this truck that could have been here a day or fifty years. It might have burned and made the flash. With all this lightning, I'm surprised there's anything left of it—yet obviously the QQB have been taking pieces of it, because . . . well, that's what they do. And if this thing on fire didn't cause the flash maybe something else did. I mean, there's no two things that are pointing in the same direction."

Again, they were all silent for a long time. They'd come a long way under some pretty shitty conditions just to end the whole affair in another riddle. Or another fuckup by the CIA. Plus, what the hell was happening back in the real world? If Armageddon had taken place already, how would they know? They were about as far away from everything as one could get.

They'd all talked it over, but really it was Gunn's call to make—flying in circles above the vast quicksand bog, unseen, unheard, but just a thousand feet above their heads.

He hated pulling the plug—but it was the right thing to do.

He was just about to give the order, when . . .

"Wait a minute!" Amanda cried out. "What *is that*?"

Everyone looked down the path, beyond where the three paratroopers were standing. A small animal was coming toward them.

"Is that a goat?" someone asked.

It walked past the paratroopers, showing no fear of them, and right up to the first tank.

It was a baby goat, gray and shaking. Amanda bent down and looked at it, petting it softly. It was obviously in a bad way, dehydrated and thin. But it showed no fear of humans.

But there was something else.

"Look at this," Amanda said to Cardillo.

She picked up the goat and held it so he could see.

He couldn't believe it.

The goat's ears had been sewn shut.

PART FOUR

CHAPTER 14

Tel Aviv

Newman needed another drink.

But it was now past midnight and he was sure that the café where he and Moon had had a couple pops earlier in the long night was closed. Plus, he surely didn't want to run into the fortune-teller again.

So he was stuck drinking bottled orange juice. It was warm, watery and bitter.

"The Israelis can turn the desert into farmland—but they can't make a good glass of orange juice?" he complained loudly.

Moon wasn't paying attention to him. His eyes were glued to his computer screen, reading updates on all the scary things happening around the world in the past few hours. Paris was indeed burning. A cadre of Hezbollah sleeper agents had emerged at the bequest of Iran to pay back the attacks on their coastal bases by the French Navy. But, incredibly, the French were continuing those attacks even as their capital was in ruins—or actually because of it. The *De Gaulle* was still launching planes and still bombing Iranian military facilities up and down the coast despite the damage done to it earlier by the suicide plane. The French were even threatening to launch an air strike on Tehran itself and were rushing more bombers, ships and troops to the region. It didn't make any sense, this *petite guerre*. It was exactly what the crisis *didn't* need. Yet it was happening, and if anything, was getting worse.

Meanwhile above the gulf, the Steel Curtain was building slowly as AWACS planes were arriving in dribs and drabs, and more and more NATO ships were entering the trouble zone. Plus, all of the international SOF units that had gathered at the Israeli desert strip were in place or would be soon—all except one. There was no word from the 201st gunship team. But that was not unexpected. They were operating under strict radio silence.

Moon looked at the clock ticking down on the lower right-hand corner of his computer screen. Only seven hours left before Israel attacked Iran.

Time was slipping away.

He turned away from the computer and saw that Newman had put aside his orange juice bottle and was back to studying the small pile of photos on his desk.

These were the images the Chinese ambassador had delivered to them earlier, the ones showing Russian MiGs flying back and forth along the Turkmenistan border. Newman had spent hours looking at them—much longer than Moon cared to. While agreeing they were odd, Moon thought it was probably just a case of the

Russians swinging their dicks at a time when they knew that every intelligence agency in the world would be looking in, except, apparently, the U.S.

But Newman had become obsessed with them—and Moon wasn't quite sure why.

"There's something here that just doesn't add up," Newman said for what seemed to be the thousandth time that night.

Moon took one long cut-and-paste from the CIA website and sent it on to the local Israeli Intell. Then he wheeled his chair over to Newman's desk.

"Want to talk about it?" he asked the senior officer.

Newman had a scratch pad full of notes.

"OK—look at this," Newman said. "We know that so far that theoretically, these suicide guys have used only Russian planes left from the ex-Iraqi air force and *not* the French ones, even though they would have been better off using the French ones. Right?"

"Check," Moon said.

"But add that to this," Newman went on. "Everyone thinks the people sending these suicide planes have their own secret agenda. But when you think about it, the bogeys are only showing up as a reaction to something."

Moon shook his head. "I don't follow . . ."

Newman referred to his massive scribbling of notes. "OK, the first five we know went after the five Iranians who wanted to play footsies with Israel. Right?"

"Right . . ." Moon agreed.

"The next attack is on the listening post at Al-za-Ash, two planes slam into it when they know we're starting to build the Steel Curtain."

"OK—go ahead . . ."

"Then the next one arrives once the *De Gaulle* is in place. And hits it."

"So?"

"So I'm beginning to think the suicide planes are not so much acting, as they are *reacting*. Causing trouble wherever and whenever it will screw things up the most. Like a chaos theory."

Newman unconsciously took a swig of his watery orange juice.

"And take it a step further," he said. "Who are these pilots, anyway? And what fighter pilot do you know who's willing to kill himself? None, *I've* ever met—they're all too much in love with themselves to want to end it all. So where are they finding these guys? Certainly not in a cave somewhere."

Moon began to say something but stopped. Actually Newman had a good point. It took a lot to train someone to fly a jet fighter.

"I mean, I guess you could say the 9/11 hijackers were the first suicide pilots," Newman went on. "But these people we're dealing with now aren't taking over a jet airliner already in flight and simply steering it into a building. These guys are *taking off* in these things. They are *flying* them to targets, they are avoiding AA, and they are hitting these targets, despite steps taken to stop them.

"Now, I know you don't have to be Chuck Yeager or the Red Baron to do these things, but it's as plain as day that these guys have some experience—and yet they are willing to kill themselves at the end of it.

"So who the hell is recruiting these nutcases? Who is training them? And where? In what airplanes? These ex-Iraqi airplanes are supposed to be rust and dust; that's what your Iranian boyfriend told you himself and that's what just about everyone who was privy to them thought. So what planes are these suicide guys training in? Plus, again, how do you teach someone to take off, fly through AA and then slam into something? You don't. These guys *have* to be experienced pilots—so where the hell are they coming from?"

Moon was paying more attention to Newman now than at any other time in the twenty years they'd known each other.

"Are they Iranian air force pilots doing this?" Newman asked after another swig of the orange-colored water. "Could that really be? If so where are their families? Where do their families think they are? If your friends in Iran *are* telling the truth, or some semblance of it, wouldn't they be all over the first person who came forward and said 'My husband the pilot is missing?'"

Newman swiveled his chair around and looked back out at the blacked-out Tel Aviv skyline.

"I'm telling you, Moonman," he said. "There's something else going on here . . ."

CHAPTER 15

Dasht-e Kavir

The goat devoured the spaghetti and meatballs.

So too the chicken à la king, the BBQ pork and the packet of freeze-dried lemonade—without the water. A tiny Snickers bar went down the gullet, without the wrapper ever coming off, as did a three-pack of gum.

The Marines finally stopped the gorging when the goat wanted to eat the plastic wrapping their MRE meals had come in.

"That might not be so good for his gut," Commander al-Kat had told them.

The 201st's ground team knew they had something here, a clue to what was happening in the middle of one of the most inhospitable places on Earth. But what was it exactly?

"Who would want a deaf goat?" Amanda had asked over and over. The team was gathered in a circle on the windswept path next to the quicksand bog. Bracketed by the pair of M1 tanks, they were trying to figure it out.

Who would want a deaf goat?

The paratrooper's medic examined the animal. Not only had his ears been sewn shut—crudely, with nothing more surgical than a common needle and thick thread—but apparently his eardrums had been punctured as well.

But again, why?

As it turned out, al-Kat knew a few things about goats. He knew by feeling the goat's nose that it was domesticated and not feral. He also knew goats were communal animals. "You see one, there are always others nearby," he said.

He also told them he wouldn't be shocked if this goat belonged to the people they were looking for, the hated QQB, and that they were nearby too. "They'll eat anything," he said of his enemies in disgust. "Bones, horns, hair."

But why would they want this animal to be deaf?

The 201st decided to find out.

IT was not an easy decision to make.

By agreeing to press on deeper into the Dasht-e Kavir, it meant the ground team was choosing to ignore their bingo point. They were committing themselves to going beyond the point of no return, and of any hope that they'd make it back to the old airfield where the AC-17, still circling endlessly above them, could pick them up. Nor could they count on anyone else rescuing them. The closest allied SOF group, the Norwegian Jegerkommandos hiding over the border in Turkmenistan, were actually more than four hundred miles away and were equipped only with transport planes, meaning they had no way to extract the 201st either, even if there was some way to contact them.

Add to this, when the sun came up in a few hours, the 201st contingent would find itself at the mercy of the most brutal heat on the planet—140 degrees Fahrenheit just an hour after sunrise. Their water supplies would go quickly, as would their food. And they, plus the orbiting C-17, would lose the cover of darkness.

All for a deaf goat.

But again, their instincts told them it meant *something*. Even Gunn, looking down from on high, admitted it.

Plus, they had one other thing going for them: Al-Kat *knew* goats.

"If goats are kept in a pen, they will find the weak spot in the fence and they will batter it until it gives way," the SSK commander told the team who were now very interested in anything they could learn about the animals. "But when they break the barrier down, while they might escape, usually all they want is to return to the safety of the pen.

"I think that's what happened here. This little one got out of a pen and became lost. But I also think he'd like to go back."

But how?

Al-Kat also knew the way to help a goat find his home. And finally, something turned out to be simple.

Al-Kat just put the animal on his shoulders and allowed it to sniff the air. The goat started crying whenever al-Kat turned to the east.

On this clue, the SSK fighter started down the wind-worn path bordering the quicksand bog, heading east. And, with Amanda, the paratroopers and the rest of the SSK fighters back on board, the two M1 tanks followed.

THEY found the second tanker truck twenty minutes later.

They'd moved off the path and back into the rugged terrain of salt hills and gullies, following al-Kat as he was following the bays of the goat. The absurdity of what they were doing started to sink in not too long into the march. The going was much slower as the M1 tank drivers could only go as fast as al-Kat could walk. Plus the wind started blowing again, and the heat lightning became more intense.

Still doing long-range scans with the balky GIR above in the AC-17, Gunn also had the rest of the paratroopers on board manning the plane's windows, looking for anything unusual on the ground via their reverse-infrared goggles.

But it was by following where the goat led them that they spotted the second truck.

It was at the bottom of a ravine about a mile from the first wreck. It was twisted and battered but more intact than the first one. It was partially covered by the blowing salt, but it was not near any quicksand, meaning the team could get right down next to it.

A gruesome discovery awaited them when they did. This truck too had been burned—along with its driver. His skeleton was still in the cab, hands grafted to the steering wheel, body melted into the seat. He'd been burned alive.

The tanker had been partially disassembled, just as the first one, but it was clear it wasn't a vehicle from the 1950s. The truck had a Toyota logo that was still recognizable on its hood. Plus it had registration tags from 2009. Amanda was able to collect a drop of liquid from the only part of the tank that hadn't burned completely.

She put the drop to her mouth and tasted it. "JP-8," she declared. "I'd know it anywhere."

That's when she pulled out her sat-phone and called Gunn circling above.

"Do you think the CIA has a satellite photo with *two* flashes on it?" she asked. "I don't . . ."

The ground team now had a little more faith in their new GPS—the "goat positioning system."

The animal had led al-Kat to the second truck and when the SSK fighter held the goat over his head again, as before, the animal started baying whenever al-Kat turned east. He began walking in that direction and again, the Americans followed.

More hills, more gullies, more wind and lots of salt. In only six hours, the sun would be up, and if events unfolded the way everyone thought they would, then come sunset, the world would be a very different place.

They moved another two miles, over more rough terrain, with the tanks' fuel supply dwindling further. More concerning, the AC-17 was now close to having fuel issues too. What would happen when *it* had to leave?

It would be basically sentencing those on the ground to death, in a hell on Earth.

And like the CIA man had said: No one would know they were gone except the scorpions.

BUT then they saw the campfires.

It was the paratroopers aboard the AC-17 who spotted them first.

They were in the middle of yet another orbit when suddenly a bright flame popped up on top of a salt mountain about three miles southeast of the ground team.

No sooner did that one appear when a second one was spotted on a hill about a quarter mile from the first. Then they saw a third, a fourth, and a fifth, all atop tall salt hills, all in a rough line. And then two more appeared, but these were on opposite sides and behind the last one.

Within thirty seconds, seven had been lit.

Gunn spotted them and said, "You've got to be kidding me . . ."

When seen from above, the fires formed an almost perfect arrow—and a crude but effective navigational aid.

He immediately called down to Amanda's sat-phone and told her what they were seeing.

"An arrow?" she replied. "But what's it pointing to? Or away from?"

No sooner were the words out of her mouth than the ground team heard an ungodly screech. Everyone hit the dirt, including al-Kat and the goat.

Two seconds later, Amanda looked over her shoulder to see two bright lights coming right at her, very low and at high speed.

Before she could react, the lights converged, the noise

became deafening and something went right over their heads.

It was a jet fighter. It materialized out of the night and went over them so low its tail almost nicked the turret of Cardillo's tank.

"Jesuzz!" several people yelled at once. The ground team was left in a cloud of thick exhaust and dust.

Everybody reacted—except the goat. It couldn't hear a thing.

"Where the hell did that come from?" Amanda yelled up to Gunn.

But before she got an answer, they heard another scream and saw two more lights, and an instant later, a second jet fighter was on them, roaring over, just as low, going just as fast, and coming just as close to hitting the raised gun barrel on the second tank.

Once again the ground team was covered with choking wet exhaust and smoke.

Gunn and his crew had spotted the second plane coming out of the gully just after it passed over the ground team. In a split second decision, Gunn tipped the huge AC-17 down on its left wing and fired off two barrages from the Vulcan cannons. The tracer streaks followed the second plane, almost catching up with its tail. But the firing angle wasn't right and the rounds fell short. The jet flew off, its pilot never knowing he'd been fired on by the huge invisible gunship.

The AC-17's gun cameras had captured video-stills of both planes, though; Gunn was looking at them seconds later. Both planes were MiG-23s. They had no country emblems, no aircraft ID numbers. Both were wearing faded camouflage color schemes.

He knew immediately these were *not* Iranian air force planes.

They were suiciders . . .

They had to be.

And they had just taken off from somewhere close by.

Gunn briefly toyed with the idea of pursuing the pair of MiGs. But if he had, he would be leaving the ground team behind to almost certain doom, as he could never chase the bogeys and still have enough gas to return to the Dasht-e Kavir and play guardian angel for his people. Plus no matter what shape they were in, if the MiGs saw him, they could still fly rings around him, could go supersonic and, if not shoot him down, then basically leave him in the dust. So he gave up on that notion pretty quickly.

He was able to follow the two planes with his reverse-infrared goggles, however, and he saw both perform a telling if extremely dangerous maneuver.

After flying very low over the salt desert, at a certain point, both planes suddenly went nose vertical. Their pilots hit their afterburners and both screamed nearly straight up until they were out of sight.

Gunn was shocked by these actions. If the ex-Iraqi planes were as brittle as everyone claimed, then this type of flying was pure insanity. Because if ever an old airplane was going to break up in flight, it would happen when a pilot hit his afterburner while going straight up. Fighting against all that gravity could tear a plane to shreds.

But at least now Gunn knew how the suicide planes had seemingly been able to appear out of nowhere. They were taking off from somewhere in the Dash, flying as low as possible and then at a predetermined point, performing their death-defying ascent to forty thousand feet or so—and only then were they picked up on radar, basically too late for anyone to do anything about it.

But suddenly none of this mattered.

Though Gunn felt helpless in that two more suicide planes were heading for targets unknown, at least now he knew where the QQB was and most likely where the mystery planes were coming from too.

All they had to do was find the other end of the arrow.

CHAPTER 16

Over the Persian Gulf

Lieutenant Bing was high as a kite.

He was moving faster than he thought possible, thinking clearer, making snap decisions, flying the big plane, looking for bad guys, watching all his screens, taking on fuel, drinking coffee, chewing gum, talking on the radio and watching real-time video of the French Navy and the Iranian Revolutionary Guards trading massive barrages of large caliber ordnance at six different locations up and down the Persian Gulf coastline.

He was also doing some reading. The ABL company rep had given him his copy of "The Falklands Factor." Bing had managed to read it cover to cover, make notes, reread some passages and even correct a few typos.

His sudden verve and vigor after being airborne for nearly twelve hours had nothing to do with healthy living or mind over matter. It had everything to do with something else the ABL guy had given him: Bennies. As in amphetamines, speed, a favorite pastime of his commanding officer, Major Gunn. Bing had been popping a couple every half hour since the suicide plane plowed into the *De Gaulle,* and damn, they made him feel good.

In fact, he'd *never* felt like this before; in the past, he'd been reluctant to even take an aspirin for a headache. But if these things were going to keep him awake and alert all night, then he was going to keep popping them. The ABL rep told him he had plenty.

There hadn't been any suicide planes since the one that hit the French aircraft carrier. But no one believed the attacks were over; no one wanted to be that optimistic. To the contrary, according to communiqués Bing was receiving directly from the Joint Chiefs, the brains in Washington believed this was a temporary lull and when morning came, the suicide planes would strike again, if not sooner.

He was flying north, making his seventh circuit of the Persian Gulf since getting on station. Below him, and stretched out beyond the horizon, he could see six separate columns of fiery smoke rising into the night. These were the Iranian naval bases at Kish, Kangan, Lavan, Bandar-e Bushehr, Dayyer and Dalara River—or what was left of them. The French Navy had utterly destroyed them all, and according to the latest CIA reports, had also flattened civilian targets near the naval bases as well.

Now, Bing received a CIA report that French ships had fired cruise missiles at the large Iranian army base at Borazjan, some fifty miles inland from the coast. If true, this was a huge escalation of the fighting between the two unlikely opponents. The CIA report noted that most of the base at Borazjan had been recently built by French companies and that its design was based on those used by the French army. The irony was as thick as the smoke in the air.

Bing's first thought was: Hezbollah will blow up the Eiffel Tower after this. As he was heading north, and was almost within view of Borazjan, he was jazzed up to see what was happening there.

But that's when he got a high-priority radio call directly from central command. As if they needed anything else to go wrong, there were now reports that an unidentified submarine had surfaced about two thirds of the way up the Persian Gulf coastline, in the area of Gene-vah-e, not five minutes' flying time from Bing's present location. The submarine was apparently in trouble, smoking heavily from the bow, and drifting toward the coast of Iran.

The problem? The sub was a Dolphin-class vessel.

And that meant it most likely belonged to the Israeli Navy. And preliminary readings said that there were radioactive elements leaking out of the sub and into the air.

In other words, it was probably carrying nuclear weapons.

HOW did an Israeli sub get into the Persian Gulf? That was another mystery.

Israel had only a few Dolphin subs, none nuclear-powered and all built by Germany. However, it was an open secret that the subs carried nuclear-tipped missiles. But Israel's sub base was on its Mediterranean coastline. How would they travel from that location to the Persian Gulf? There was no way an Israeli sub was going to sail through the Suez Canal. That would be like sailing through the middle of Egypt. And going out the Med, into the Atlantic, around Africa and up that way would take weeks.

So, how did it get there so quickly? The only explanation was one suggested by an Israeli novelist years before that claimed Israel had specially built vessels disguised as cargo ships that could actually carry Dolphin submarines in their cargo holds and deliver them anywhere in the world.

But however it got into the gulf, it was now in trouble, extremely vulnerable and drifting closer to Iranian waters by the minute.

Then came the second piece of bad news from central command. The AWACS fleet had picked up two bogeys coming out of Iran and they were suddenly heading southwest, not toward Israel but toward the disabled submarine. In fact they were but forty miles away from the sub at the moment and coming on fast.

No one had to say what this meant. If the suicide planes managed to crash into the Israeli sub, then whoever was sending them on these missions wouldn't have to hit Israel anymore. Destroying one of their nuclear-armed subs would be just as good. If that happened, the nuked-up Israeli fighter bombers would be off their runways in a matter of minutes.

Central command's message to Bing then was very clear: It was up to him and his airplane's balky lasers to stop the suiciders before they crashed into the sub and finally lit off World War III.

On hearing the news, Bing popped two more Bennies and crammed five new sticks of gum into his mouth.

Then he addressed his crew of civilian contractors.

"OK, guys," he said. "Let's rock and roll . . ."

BY the time Bing's radar man picked up the two bogeys, they were just twenty miles away and coming on fast.

Bing had already found the crippled sub below. He had gone into an orbit around the stricken vessel and was amazed it was still afloat—it was smoking that heavily.

The chief ABL company rep was already up in the C-17's top turret. He'd activated the weapon, and as a result, everything inside the C-17 had dimmed considerably, including the plane's Star Skin.

Bing was moving at super-human speed now—or at least it seemed to him like he was. He knew the ABL shooter was already speeding like mad, and he was hoping that between the two of them they could knock out the pair of suicide planes—and do it quickly!

"I got a bead," the ABL shooter yelled down to Bing. "We are ranging good and there is no weather in the way."

Bing checked his situation read-out screen. The two suicide planes were now fifteen miles away and descending. Meanwhile, he was maintaining his altitude of fifty-five hundred feet.

"OK, fire it!" Bing yelled up to the shooter.

An instant later, he heard the sizzle of the generator in the back of the plane and then the distinctive crackle.

But then came a loud *pop!*

Then nothing.

The ABL shooter yelled down to him: "Fuck! It must have short-circuited . . ."

"Try the other one," Bing yelled back at him.

The shooter dropped out of the turret, through the flight deck, and to the nose laser bubble.

Bing looked at his radar screen. The two bogeys were now ten miles away, diving through twenty thousand feet and heading right at the sub—with only his C-17 separating them.

"OK," the shooter said. "I got a lock . . ."

"Then fire the goddamn thing!" Bing cried.

The shooter activated the ABL's trigger; and once again, everything electrical aboard the plane dimmed. They heard the generator in back sizzle and crackle.

But again, nothing happened. No red glow. No flash of the laser beam burst from the twin tubes. Not even a pop this time.

"Jesus—damn—Jessuz!" Bing heard the shooter cry.

"Is it a power drain problem?" he yelled to the shooter.

"It could be a million things," the guy yelled back.

Bing started hitting off switches. He was killing all nonessential electrical systems, including the plane's Star Skin. Just like that, they were no longer invisible.

"Try it again!" he yelled to the shooter.

For the third time, the man squeezed the laser's trigger—and for the third time it failed to fire.

Bing didn't even think about his next move. He reacted purely on instinct, aided by the chemicals running through his bloodstream. There was no way the bogeys could hit the sub. If that happened, then the war would be on. Israel would push the button, and they'd all be toast.

So he pulled up on the controls and aimed the big plane right at the two oncoming suicide planes.

Eight miles away and closing fast.

"Try it again!" he yelled.

The whole sequence happened again. The shooter hit the trigger, everything dimmed, the generator crackled and sizzled—and then nothing.

The pair of suicide planes was still coming right at them, square on. Bing wondered if they could even see him in the dark. He increased power to his engines, and stayed steady on the control stick. But this was getting very hairy. Playing chicken with people who were planning to kill themselves anyway was no great sport.

Suddenly Bing was furious. He thought, *Damn, I'm going to die protecting those assholes and their sub . . .*

He was also mad at himself. It was that fucking "Falklands Factor" report. He wished he'd never read the damn thing because *everything* it predicted was coming true, right before his eyes.

"Try it again!" he yelled to the ABL guy.

Again, the shooter hit the trigger, again everything on the plane dimmed. Again, nothing else happened.

"The fucking thing is crapped out . . ." the shooter yelled.

Bing couldn't believe this was happening. He was

less than a minute away from a midair collision with two MiGs that didn't look like they were going to veer out of the way.

What the fuck can I do?

"Try the other one again," he yelled to the company rep. "Up top!"

"But that one is busted too!" the guy yelled back.

"Just try the fucking thing!" Bing screamed at him.

The guy didn't respond. He just jumped up from the nose turret, scrambled up through the flight deck, stuck his head into the top turret and turned it back on.

"I got a bead and . . ." he started to say.

Bing cut him off. "Just shoot the fucking thing!"

This time, everything happened at once. The electricals dimmed, the generator crackled and sizzled—but then the red glow enveloped the cockpit and the laser shot out of the top turret.

The ABL finally worked . . .

Bing actually saw the beam hit the lead suicide plane. That's how close they were. It went through the cockpit and took the pilot's head right off. The suicide plane twisted away and headed straight down, plummeting to the Persian Gulf below.

The shooter then manually turned the turret and fired at the second bogey. The ABL worked this time too—but the bogey was right on them. The laser pierced the plane's center fuel tank. It exploded in an instant, tearing the jet's tail off.

The MiG went hard left; Bing went hard right—but it was impossible to avoid a collision. The MiG slammed into the C-17's left wing, taking half of it with it. The

C-17 rolled over instantly and started heading straight down.

Suddenly multiple alarms were sounding in the cockpit. Smoke was everywhere. Bing was upside down and pulling three g's. Then four. What was happening? They were all seconds away from death.

He was looking down at the dark water coming up at him extremely fast. It was like a bad dream, or more accurately, someone *else's* bad dream.

He knew he had about five seconds to think and then it would be too late. That's when he remembered his old paratrooper trick—how he was able to get his big plane to almost hover in the air. That's what he needed. But would it work if the plane was upside down?

He had to try. He extended his landing gear, dropped his movable slats and pulled back on the throttles, all at the same time. As a result, he was instantly going nose down, but at reduced airspeed. He frantically increased power and with all his might tried to pull the nose up. And incredibly, it worked—the plane stopped dropping and started to level off. He kept pulling on the controls and a few moments later he was back to what resembled level flight.

For about two seconds . . .

Because now the plane started to roll over to the left.

Bing's hands started moving before his brain did. He killed the outboard engine on the wounded wing and increased power to the inboard one. Then he pushed the controls all the way to the right.

Once more, the plane shuddered violently, but to his amazement he leveled out again.

He was so shook up by this time, he was instantly bathed in sweat. He looked behind him and saw the crew was on the cabin floor, battered, bloody, unconscious; a few possibly dead, including the ABL shooter. None of them were in any shape to help him. Plus he was flying without a copilot. He was doing this all himself.

Only one thing was for certain: He had to find someplace to set down.

Fighting the controls with one hand, he started punching his flight computer with the other, even as the flight deck began filling with smoke. Somehow he was able to come up with a map of the area showing airports, landing strips and military bases. The bad news was the nearest bases were all in Iran. He didn't think they'd appreciate him dropping in.

The nearest nonenemy base was fifty miles west across the gulf near Khafji in Saudi Arabia.

God—how am I going to fly fifty miles in this condition?

Then the C-17 shuddered once again.

Bing looked out his cockpit window just in tine to see a large section of skin on his partially severed left wing rip itself off. It tumbled backward and crashed into the C-17's high tail, severing it in half.

"God damn . . ."

The plane started plunging again; Bing yanked back on the controls, increased power and reduced the dive. But he was still losing altitude and now he was going sideways.

It was about that time his flight controls just stopped working. His stick went completely dead. So did two of his throttle bars. He immediately switched seats—only to find that while the copilot stick worked, the foot pedals did not.

It is happening, he thought, recalling "The Falklands Factor" report. Things were going wrong, and the more complicated the thing was, the more likely it was to break. Bing cursed himself again for ever picking up the gloomy document. Basically it was just a prelude of his obituary.

What's the point of this? he thought, looking over his shoulder again, and seeing the bloody and broken pile of bodies behind him. *If it's all going for naught anyway, then why the fuck try?* Fate had intervened and they were all going to die and everything he was doing was just forestalling the inevitable. He couldn't *be* in both seats at the same time—the final Falklands Factor curse. Thus, they were screwed.

But then something came to him. The huge airplane was tumbling out of the sky; it was on fire and he was losing all his flying surfaces as well as his ability to reach the working controls—and yet an idea popped into his head as if he'd been hit by lightning. Or an empty champagne bottle.

He reached behind him, grabbed the hardcover folder that contained the ABL guy's copy of "The Falklands Factor" . . . and jammed it behind the working foot pedal on the pilot's side. Then he returned to the copilot's station and began working the stick and throttles.

Incredibly, the big plane leveled out. It was shaky, it was noisy, but Bing held it like this for the next ten minutes, muscles breaking, blood coming from his ears and mouth, blood vessels bursting all over his face. Oily smoke was going up his nose, fouling his eyes, but still he held on, and eventually the airport on the Saudi coastal city of Khafji came into view.

He tried the radio—and surprise! The damn thing worked.

He explained his situation to the air traffic controller, who spoke perfect English, and he was given immediate clearance to land—like he had any other choice.

He hit the runway going 222 knots—usually a death sentence but not now, not here, because this airfield happened to be an alternative safety diversion site for U.S. heavy bombers deployed here during the first Gulf War. The runway, which ran right along the edge of the water, was more than four miles long.

He blew out more than half of his tires on touchdown, and his left inboard engine fell off one third of the way into the landing roll, but gradually Bing began to slow down, and eventually he pulled the huge smoldering plane to a stop.

He killed the engines and then just sat there. He was not shaking. He was bloody but not sweating anymore. In fact, he was laughing.

The Saudi rescue personnel arrived seconds later. They flooded aboard the plane and sprayed him and everyone on it with Purple K fire repellant. Bing helped carry the eleven injured men out of the airplane and into the waiting ambulances. Some were seriously injured, but all would live to see another day.

Once they were gone, Bing returned to the cockpit and pulled out the copy of "The Falklands Factor" that he had jammed behind his working foot pedals. He climbed back down to the runway, walked to the edge and, with a mighty toss, threw the book into the turbulent waters of the Persian Gulf nearby. He watched it float away and finally sink.

Then he wiped his hands and said, "That takes care of that."

CHAPTER 17

Dasht-e Kavir

The pool of water shimmered in the suddenly tranquil night. The sky had cleared of clouds and the stars were out in full force. They were so numerous they seemed close enough to touch. A gentle wind rustled the branches on the oasis's fig trees. Other than that, and a few bursts of heat lightning to the north, it was quiet.

Atop a nearby embankment, four pairs of reverse-infrared goggles looked down on the scene. Other than a slight reflection off these goggles, the top of the embankment appeared empty. That's because four people lying there were invisible.

They were Amanda, Cardillo, al-Kat and one of the paratroopers. They were all wearing Mag-cloaks. The SSK man couldn't believe they'd become invisible. Amanda was holding the goat tight.

They had followed the end of the campfires to this spot on the embankment. It was about forty feet high and had a 180-degree field of view. To the right was the open salty desert. To the left, a long patch of weeds with some large rocks mixed in that stretched for at least a mile, maybe more.

In front of them was the salt mountain. Easily a thousand feet high, it had a sheer face on the near side and ran parallel to the rocky weed patch for almost its entire length. One of the campfires was still smoldering on its peak.

Down in front of them was the oasis. It was a small pool with four olive trees clustered on one side, located very close to the side of the mountain. The goat pen was about twenty feet to its right.

And that's all that was here.

No air base. No runway. Certainly no jet fighters. Just the goats, the water and the olive trees.

Amanda set the goat free. It ran down the side of the embankment and with amazing agility, leapt over the rickety wooden fence and right back in the middle of the herd of goats, most of whom were asleep. The young goat made a ruckus, jumping up and down to get the attention of the others. They'd had their ears sewn shut too. Once they realized he was back, many came over to sniff him then lick his face, before going back to sleep. The wayward goat settled in between a few of the larger goats and went to sleep too, his escape and adventure already forgotten.

Amanda called up to Gunn.

"This *must* be the place," she told him. "Because this is where the campfires end. But it's so . . . *quiet*."

"Do you think I should drop the groceries?" Gunn asked her. "Once they're down there's no picking them back up."

Amanda took another long look around. Except for the deaf goats and the smoldering campfire, there was nothing suspicious or extraordinary about this place at all.

She looked over at Cardillo. The Marine officer scanned the scene again through his goggles but just shrugged.

"It's where the animal led us," he said. "And *someone* lit that fire up there. But other than that . . ."

Suddenly they heard a noise. All four people up on the embankment froze. Something was happening down near the oasis.

But what?

The fig trees started shaking. The pool water began rippling more intensely. The wind even picked up a little. Only the goats didn't move.

There was a strange grinding noise, and then the side of the salt mountain opened up.

It was a hidden door. At least twenty-five feet long and built right into the side of the salt mountain, it looked not unlike a regular garage door, only bigger.

A lone man walked out from under it, holding a pail and carrying a torch. He made his way over to the goat pen, climbed inside, rousted one of the larger goats and calmly went about milking it.

While this was happening, Amanda and the others turned their attention back to the open door and the chamber they could see that lay on the other side of it. It was dark inside this chamber, and hot outside, which did not help when viewing it through the goggles. But some things were evident. There were definitely airplanes within—in fact the chamber was more accurately described as a hangar, because many planes were apparent in its cool shadows and at a quick glance, most of them looked like old Russian-designed fighters, the exact same planes as the suicide pilots flew.

Also inside, right near the northern edge of the moving door, there was a sort of indoor junkyard. There were many piles of scrap metal here, scrap metal that looked to Amanda like pieces of airplanes.

They only had a tantalizingly brief glimpse into the hangar, though, because after only a minute or so, the man milking the goat had filled his pail. He climbed back out of the pen, walked by the oasis and went through the door again. The door came back down, it's façade matching perfectly to the sheer side of the mountain.

Amanda turned to Cardillo and whispered, "Please tell me you just saw all that."

"I'm not sure I believe it," the Marine officer replied. "But yes, I did."

Amanda let out a long breath of relief. "At least we *are* in the right place," she said.

She called back up to Gunn.

"This is where we want to be," she told him. "So, yes, drop off the groceries."

A minute later, the four people on the embankment heard a whooshing sound go over their heads.

The sky was still clear, but almost imperceptibly, many dark shapes appeared against the starry background and silently drifted to Earth. Another minute passed, and then the area behind the embankment was suddenly teeming with 82nd Airborne paratroopers.

Twenty in all had been dropped by the AC-17; the complement of paratroopers on the ground was now an even two dozen. Linking up with the rest of the SSK fighters, they joined Amanda, Cardillo and the others hiding up on the ridge.

SO the hangar was hidden inside the salt mountain. Gunn couldn't believe it after Amanda told him. They'd seen some interesting displays of camouflage in the 201st's brief career. Their training base in Nevada was covered with the amazing electromagnetic camouflage netting, just like the hidden government base in the Pine Barrens of New Jersey. In their first combat mission, the 201st had battled a terrorist army that had holed up inside a huge mountain in the wilds of northern Pakistan, more than a thousand fighters, completely hidden from view. That complex had been carved out of natural caves and caverns, which had all been connected, making the mountain habitable. During their African adventure, Gunn and Amanda had discovered an al Qaeda hideout buried in the side of a cliff in the middle of the deepest jungle on the Dark Continent.

But neither of these last two places had a door, never mind a gigantic, movable door.

He flew over the mountain now and turned on his wounded GIR scanner. The device was just too damaged to give him a good reading, but even in the safe mode, he was able to "see" a little bit into the side of the mountain.

The hangar, and the huge chamber it was contained in, appeared to have been dug out of pure salt by hand. The edges weren't finished, as they might have been had a boring machine been used. Rather, the sides had been chipped away precisely, as if a sculptor had done the work. By opening the door, a whole little world was revealed inside. By closing it, everything just blended into the landscape.

Even to the see-all eye of a spy satellite, or a spy plane, all this would have proved impossible to discern, except from ground level. And the fact that it was located literally out in the middle of nowhere only added to its defense against any kind of detection. It was mastery in deception and concealment.

"How long has this thing been here?" Gunn found himself thinking aloud.

"These QQB guys are pretty smart," Lieutenant Mike Robinson, his flight engineer and temporary copilot, said. "For guys who live out in the middle of the desert, that is."

Gunn could only agree. "Too smart, if you ask me."

His sat-phone beeped again.

It was Amanda. "Something new is happening down here," she said to him in a whisper.

"Remain in place," Gunn told her. "And stay cool . . ."

WHAT happened was the huge door had opened again and this time, several dozen men, apparently QQB fighters, walked out of the chamber. They were all holding torches.

"How many people does that place hold?" Amanda

whispered to Cardillo. The total ground team was under thirty people. Another forty were still up in the AC-17. But almost a hundred people had just walked out of the chamber—and many more could still be seen inside.

"The QQB have always outnumbered us," al-Kat whispered to Amanda. "And they must be gaining new recruits."

About eighty of the men broke off from this group and walked out to the long rocky, weedy field. Very systematically, they started rolling, pushing, lifting and moving the hundreds of rocks that littered the long narrow stretch of land. It was sheer manpower, plus it was obvious they'd done this sort of thing before. Inside of ten minutes, they had transformed the weedy field into a rough, but serviceable runway.

"The Chinese used to do the same thing at their bases during World War Two," Robinson said, watching along with Gunn through his goggles. "You can do a lot—with a lot of muscle."

Once done, the men extinguished their torches and then sat down in specific places on either side of the cleared land. That part of the hidden base suddenly went dark.

Now, another couple dozen men came out of the hidden hangar. They were pushing a jet fighter—a MiG-23 Flogger. They were moving it in the direction of the weedy runway. Their way was also being lit by torches.

"Damn—we got one," Gunn whispered, seeing all this.

He called down to Amanda. "Everyone *stay cool*. See what they're up to first."

Those hiding on the ground and those hiding in the

air expected the same thing: that the people pushing the airplane would move it to the newly-exposed runway, load its wings down with high explosives or worse, and prepare it for takeoff.

But that isn't what happened.

Rather, to their astonishment, the QQB fighters turned the MiG backward, so it faced the junkyard hidden in the far side of the chamber. Then instead of rolling out a cart full of dynamite, a tool cart was pushed out of the hangar. It contained an acetylene torch and dozens of manual cutting tools like hacksaws. Once in place, up to three dozen of the QQB fighters took these tools and proceeded to cut the MiG-23 into pieces. Within just a couple minutes, the big fighter plane was on its way to becoming a pile of junk.

"What the heck is going on here?" Amanda asked Gunn via the cell phone.

Gunn was just as perplexed. What they were watching didn't make sense. Why would the QQB fighters be reducing the airplane to scrap? Wasn't it supposed to take off and go slam into something?

"Check out the guy with the torch," Robinson told him.

Everyone's eyes went to the man holding the acetylene torch. He was wearing a crude welder's mask, but no other protective clothing. As his colleagues continued to saw into the MiG-23's wings, fuselage and tail, this man placed a ladder against the fighter's nose, climbed to its top step, then using the torch, cut out a square section of the nose located just in front of the cockpit. Like a ham-fisted surgeon, he removed this panel, reached in and took out an instrument the size of a car battery. It was painted orange.

"Is that the black box?" Robinson asked.

By this time, the rest of the MiG was basically in pieces. Its wings, tail and nosecone were gone. Its engines had dropped to the ground and chains were being wrapped around them. Then, the torch man, who seemed to be in charge, barked an order to the QQB fighters. They started picking up pieces of the MiG and carrying them to the indoor junkyard. The two huge engines were dragged there as well. Others fighters were digging through the pile of electronics they'd managed to take out of the plane, apparently looking for valuable components. In less than fifteen minutes, the small army of QQB fighters had essentially made the MiG-23 disappear.

"OK," Gunn said. "Can *anybody* tell me what the hell is going on?"

But before he got an answer, the campfires started up again.

And then the AC-17's air defense radar began buzzing.

"What's this?" Robinson asked their crew.

"We've got a bogey coming in from due east," the gunship's weapons officer told him. "Unsteady in altitude. Acting very weird."

With the push of a button, Gunn was looking at the radar intercept screen on his own flight panel.

He quickly understood what his weapons officer was talking about. He too could see the bogey's signature going on and off the screen. It was flying so erratically, it took Gunn a few moments to figure out what was going on.

Then he realized the bogey was flying very low in between the mountains that dominated the terrain east of the hidden hangar. Some of these mountains ran all the way back to the eastern border of Iran and beyond. Twisting and turning in between these high peaks, the bogey was reaching high subsonic speeds, and trying its best to stay off anybody's radar. It certainly would not be picked up by ground-based radar—the mountains prevented that. It was only because Gunn's C-17 carried such a highly advanced look-down radar that the bogey had been spotted at all.

But it *was* acting weirdly. Its profile indicated that it was a MiG-23 Flogger, oddly the same type of airplane that the QQB fighters had just reduced to scrap.

They watched the bogey for the next few minutes until it was within two miles of the hidden base.

"Everyone continue to stay down," Gunn cautioned them again. "Let's see what happens next."

"So, just as one is pulled apart," Robinson said, "another one shows up? It doesn't make sense."

They continued watching the bogey as it bounced up and down, weaving in and out of the twisting mountain passes, going treacherously fast.

Once it was one mile from the QQB base, something else happened. Those several dozen QQB fighters arrayed on the runway stood up, relit their torches and held them high. And now at least one aspect of all this was clear: the QQB fighters were basically serving as human runway lights.

The bogey came up and over the last mountain and landed, in the dim shadowy conditions, bouncing in on the rough, grassy runway.

Gunn was trying hard to put the puzzle together. Why was this plane flying around out there? Was it a pilot in training? Why would the QQB be tearing apart a plane just like the one that just landed? And what about the two planes they'd seen take off about an hour earlier?

The bogey finally came into view. It was indeed a MiG-23, exactly like the plane that had just been reduced to junk. It taxied right up to the open door of the chamber, rumbling by the deaf goats, who hardly noticed. Thus, another question was answered. With all the jets coming and going, the goats had to be made deaf so they wouldn't freak out from all the engine noise.

As the 201st team watched, the MiG turned a 180. Six men carrying a fuel hose from the mountain chamber appeared; inside they could now see a third tanker truck. The hose was attached to the recently landed MiG and it started to be refueled.

Then the man in charge appeared again. He was carrying his ladder and the black box that he'd just removed from the plane that had been reduced to junk. He leaned the ladder against the nose of the newly-arrived MiG, removed an access panel, and essentially dropped the black box inside. Then he screwed the access panel back on and signaled the pilot.

His refueling done, the pilot gunned his engines even before the ladder could be taken away. The jet fighter started rolling toward the bumpy runway, nearly running over the man in charge.

And the plane never stopped moving. There was a bright flash as the pilot hit his afterburners and began rocketing down the bumpy runway at an incredible speed.

"Did you see that flash?" Amanda cried into her cell phone. "The CIA sat photo had been right all along!"

But beyond that, none of this made sense to Gunn or anyone else. All he knew was that another suicide plane was taking off to hit another target.

"Jessuz!" he yelled. "We've got to stop that plane!"

The MiG was halfway down the runway by this time. But then the Marines' second tank, which had taken its place at the end of the improvised landing strip earlier, squeaked itself into view, lowered its gun muzzle and fired. The tank shell hit the MiG square on the nose just as its wheels were leaving the ground. The plane exploded in a ball of flame, obliterated from the point-blank shot. Its debris cloud kept on moving and rained down upon the tank, hot smoking pieces bouncing off of it everywhere.

That's when all hell broke loose.

Stunned by the sudden destruction of the MiG, the armed QQB fighters began firing in all directions at once. Some of this gunfire found itself going in the direction of the Marine tank that was now out on the runway and helplessly exposed.

So, on Gunn's call, the paratroopers and the SSK fighters atop the embankment opened up on those QQB fighters near the entrance to the hangar who were firing at the tank. Surprised by this sudden return fire from nowhere, this crowd of QQB fighters split in two. Half ran back toward the hidden hangar. The others, cut off from the entrance by the paratroopers' barrage, turned as one and tried to escape into the open desert to the south.

Meanwhile, the large group of armed men who were holding torches out on the improvised runway were now caught in the cross fire, as the Marine tank began shooting toward the chamber, and some of the people down near the chamber were shooting back. Their torches extinguished, it was almost completely dark again at the hidden base, only adding to the panic.

That's when the AC-17 appeared overhead.

Gunn opened up on the men on the runway with his Vulcan cannons and the CIWS gun. The rounds tore into them like a tidal wave. Any QQB fighter within the long, narrow strip of land was cut down instantly. For one horrible macabre moment, it appeared the victims were dancing among the rain of fire coming down on them. Four seconds was all it took. None of them were left standing when it was over.

The big gunship then banked hard left. Gunn sighted a concentration of fleeing fighters very close to making it inside the mountain chamber. He hit the weapons engage button; his trio of Gatling guns opened up. The barrage obliterated this cluster of men.

A second group nearby was more scattered than the first, and now they were running in full-blown terror. Gunn let loose with two of his Vulcan cannons, a couple seconds' burst from both; again, that's all it took. The shells tore into the fleeing men, mowing most of them down.

Those few QQB fighters lucky enough to escape that barrage were doing everything they could to get back to the hangar, confused as to how this rain of fire had so suddenly come out of the clear night sky. That's when

Cardillo's tank, stationed up on the ridge, opened fire, cutting them down with tank shells and machine-gun bullets.

Thus, the slaughter continued.

MEANWHILE, the *other* group of QQB fighters, the ones that had fled into the desert, had stopped and were now regrouping on the opposite side of the mountain. It would not be good if these men were allowed to scatter. Terrorists left unkilled just meant terrorists who would terrorize at a later date. Or maybe they were planning a counterattack on the outnumbered 201st ground team.

Either way they had to be dealt with.

So Gunn jerked the big gunship to the left, nearly standing it up on its left wing, and pushed the throttle forward. This was not the way the gunship was designed to be flown, and he knew it, but he had no other choice. He was quickly over the large concentration of fighters and let go with everything he had.

All sixteen of his weapons fired at once—knocking the big jet nearly a hundred feet in the air, the recoil was that bad at such a sharp angle. At the same moment, the glare of all the weapons firing was picked up by the sensors embedded in the plane's Star Skin, magnifying the frightening flash one hundredfold.

It blinded Gunn and Robinson to the point that for a few perilous seconds, neither of them could see. The plane started to lose its flight envelope and began to stall. Its engines screamed in protest, as the extremely sharp turn continued.

Somehow Gunn recovered, and a second later Robinson could see again as well, and they both pulled on the plane's controls trying to right the enormous, airborne man-of-war.

Twenty very tense seconds passed, as the AC-17 came very close to falling out of the air. But somehow Gunn and Robinson got it back under their control and leveled off at seven hundred feet. Then they looked down at what they had wrought: there was a gigantic smoking hole where the retreating fighters had gathered and it was filled with bodies.

"As advertised," Robinson said darkly.

THOSE QQB fighters that had managed to survive the 201st's onslaught were now running, crawling or staggering back toward the mountain hangar.

But suddenly standing in their way was the line of paratroopers from the embankment. The airborne troops had tried to encircle the fighters in an effort to prevent any of them from getting back into the chamber. But because there were many more of the QQB fighters than anyone could have imagined, these paratroopers were suddenly in danger of being surrounded themselves.

"God damn," Gunn cursed, seeing it from above. "This is not good . . ."

That's when Cardillo's tank came rumbling down the embankment. With the SSK fighters and Amanda back on board, they started firing at the regrouped QQB fighters. But although the tank was moving faster than ever before, it was actually a few seconds too late. Holding tightly on to the turret, Amanda could see a disaster was in the making. The paratroopers had found themselves caught between the stampede of QQB fighters intent on getting back underneath the mountain and the open hangar door. But within the hangar, were even more QQB fighters, and they were starting to shoot out at the paratroopers as well.

In other words, the paratroopers were under the QQB's guns no matter which way they went. Plus they were in too close quarters for the gunship overhead to attempt a saving barrage.

But somehow, Cardillo's driver was able to hurl the tank into the open space separating the paratroopers from the QQB fighters rushing to get back into the mountain, at the same time, firing its machine guns into the chamber itself, countering those QQB fighters inside who were firing out. Those paratroopers who were able to used the distraction to return to higher ground.

But one trooper, caught in the middle, took a spray of bullets in the legs. Cardillo ordered the tank stopped and the paratrooper was somehow able to drag himself up onto the back. Amanda immediately crawled out of the secondary turret and reached out for him. He caught her hand and hung on as the tank started turning a 180. But by now, the QQB fighters running for the hangar were right on top of them. The tank had no choice but to turn around again, go in reverse and back up full speed into the hangar itself, all while firing its machine guns and its cannon at the onrushing gunmen.

But the moment the tank was inside, someone hit the controls and the big door started to shut.

Amanda had pulled the paratrooper up to the turret just as the tank had entered the chamber. Suddenly everything went dark. Only then did she spin around and realize what was happening. The QQB fighters had shut the gigantic door behind them.

Just like that, the tank was trapped inside.

GUNN had seen everything—and was suddenly beside himself.

He twisted the big plane around again, trying to get a better view of what was happening below. He knew it was selfish, but he was praying that the tank he'd just seen drive into the hangar was the same one that destroyed the suicide plane taking off.

Because Amanda was in the other one.

But his heart sank when he saw the second Marine tank charging down the runway, going across the landing strip past the burning remains of the MiG it had just blown to pieces.

"Jesus—damn!" Gunn cried. He pushed the big plane into yet another wildly inappropriate turn, trying to get it pointing in the right direction, so the entrance to the cave was on his left. He saw some stray QQB fighters running below him and he almost offhandedly opened up on them with the CIWS gun.

He flew past the mountain, looked at the cave door through his reverse-infrared goggles, but he knew that he couldn't risk throwing a broadside at the portal. Or even hit it with his artillery or his Bofors. There was too much of a chance that such a barrage would collapse the entire hangar and kill everyone trapped inside.

But there was no way he was going to stay up here—not when Amanda was trapped down there.

He yelled back to the people riding in the cargo bay. "We're going to land!"

Everyone on board was stunned—none so much as his copilot Lieutenant Robinson.

"You sure, Major?" he asked, looking down at the very narrow airstrip. "That place is narrow, just for little jets. We might make it down, but once we're down there, we might not make it back out."

Gunn didn't care. "We'll figure it out later," he said, putting the AC-17 into a sharp dive. "Let's prepare for landing."

IT took a few moments for everyone inside Cardillo's tank to realize the situation they found themselves in.

Like a freeze frame, no one moved after the big door shut behind them. Amanda scanned the inside of the hangar for an instant. It was dark, dank and even foggy. She saw airplanes and tools and guns and crates of ammunition, but she also saw bizarre things like hundreds of boxes containing sneakers, and dead animals, some squashed on the floor, others hanging from the ceiling. She saw the third tanker truck with the body of a man who must have been the driver hanging over it from a rafter. And everywhere, empty medication vials, tiny bottles that no doubt had once contained Adrenalin, morphine, or worse and a sea of hypodermic needles. Put all together, it was like a vision from a nightmare.

Then . . . eyes began popping up through the shadows. Like Morlocks from an H. G. Wells story, they belonged to the QQB and they too were just realizing what had happened. Now, they were inching forward, growling, grunting. Making horrible sounds, these people were in T-shirts and jeans and wearing sneakers, all of them brutal, filthy and bloody.

Then, suddenly, the bullets started flying again.

It was hard to tell who was shooting at whom. The SSK fighters had fallen or jumped off the tank, but the wounded paratrooper was still there with Amanda. Cardillo reached down and in one motion, pulled Amanda headfirst into the tank. Then he grabbed the wounded paratrooper and pulled him inside also, cramming him on top of Amanda. At the same moment, there was an explosion on the left side of the tank—a hand grenade maybe. Three pieces of burning shrapnel came zinging through the tank's portside observation slot, hitting the M1's weapon loader in the chest. He slumped forward, further pinning Amanda to the floor of the tank.

It was pitch-black inside the M1 and Amanda could barely see Cardillo, just a few feet above her, frantically firing his turret-mounted .50-caliber machine gun. When it ran out of ammunition, he began firing his M4, and when that was expended, he grabbed the wounded paratrooper's M4 and started firing that. She could see arms and legs and hands reaching out, trying to grab Cardillo and pull him out of the tank. Amanda twisted around in the darkness, grabbed onto Cardillo's legs and hung on. This way she prevented at least one person from pulling the Marine officer out of the tank.

She held on as tight as she could—but finally heard the M4 Cardillo was firing run out of ammunition. The Marine then fought the QQB fighters off using the rifle like a club, Amanda still holding on tight to his legs. Finally Cardillo pulled himself free of the attackers, fell down inside the tank, and slammed the turret hatch after him.

Without missing a beat, Cardillo came up with his sidearm and started firing it through the forward observation slot.

Through all this, Amanda still couldn't move; she was crammed so far down inside the tank. She didn't know where her M4 was, and she couldn't twist or turn enough to get to her sidearm.

It seemed like there were ten people jammed inside the tank, not just six. Smoke was filling the compartment. The noise was incredible.

Cardillo was yelling, "Stay down! Stay down! It will be OK!" as he was firing his handgun through the forward slot.

Meanwhile, the tank's driver was frantically trying to maneuver the huge machine, but it was impossible. Amanda had a cockeyed view of what was going on outside as she found herself pressed up against the side viewing slot. The SSK fighters and the QQB were locked in mortal combat, slashing one another with knives, bashing one another with rifle butts. Blood was being splattered everywhere, the sounds of gunshots and screaming were deafening.

All the while, the tank driver was spinning the huge machine round and round. He was knocking over QQB fighters, pieces of airplanes and boxes of sneakers. Amanda could see the QQB fighters being thrown off the tank, like lions attacking a bucking wildebeest. Three or four would be thrown off, only to have three or four more jump on. Some were being shot off by Cardillo and the driver firing their weapons out the vents. But the QQB fighters were fanatical. They were ripping equipment off the outside of the tank, as if they were intent on tearing the tank apart, piece by piece, with their bare hands.

Amanda made another attempt to find her M4, but it was no good; she was helpless. Suddenly she saw a shaft of dull red light enter the tank. To her horror, the tank's rear loading hatch had been yanked open. Hands were reaching in to grab her. She turned to see the face of a monster, a QQB fighter, dirty, drooling laughing and bleeding—he had grabbed her by the ankles and was pulling her out of the tank! She frantically tried to get to her sidearm, but it was impossible. She was too frightened to scream—it was all happening so fast. The man had her halfway out the hatch when suddenly she saw his eyes go wide. A knife went across his throat. The color drained from his face in an instant and he fell away, to be replaced by a familiar face.

It was al-Kat.

"I protect God's angels!" he shouted to her.

But in the next second, she saw a bullet slice his face in two.

Then the hatch was slammed and the tank turned once more.

With the horrible vision of al-Kat's bloody face burned into her retinas, Amanda was in the dark again.

GUNN was going to attempt a landing that would break every rule in the book.

He had to come in with the wind, instead of into it.

He wouldn't be able to use his rocket assists as they were now almost out of fuel and if he ever wanted to get out of this place, he had to hope he had enough left to help the AC-17 get off the ground again. All of this might have been moot though, because he wasn't even sure if his wings would clear the west side of the salt mountain, or the east side of the embankment.

None of this made any difference to him, though, not really. He quickly overflew the embankment again, letting the rest of the paratroopers jump so they would survive if he fucked up the landing. He told his flight crew they should jump too. Robinson agreed to stay, though, to help him with the landing.

All this happened very quickly. Not a minute after the tank became trapped inside the hidden chamber, Gunn was turning on his final approach for landing.

He came in low over the far end of the salt mountain, trying to drain off as much speed as possible. He had the plane close to stalling speed at this point. With Robinson looking out the right-hand window at the embankment and Gunn looking left at the mountain, they both used their combined experience to set the huge plane down in the narrow passageway.

It was a rough touchdown, lots of banging and swerving. But somehow they got the big plane to slow down. Gunn screeched it to a stop, skidding right up to the closed hidden hangar door.

By this point, the recently dropped paratroopers had linked up with the squad that had been saved by the first tank. The other tank was also on the scene, after quickly getting off the runway to allow the AC-17 to bounce in. Gunn and Robinson jumped out of the AC-17 almost before it stopped rolling. Now they had a substantial force on their side of the door—but how to get in? The door was tight and flush right up against the mountain.

What was horrible, though, was they could clearly hear the screams and gunshots of a terrible battle going on inside. Gunn was freaking out. He started clawing his way into the chamber—by hand.

But then, three things happened, almost simultaneously.

Robinson had retreated to the AC-17 and returned with a device that looked like a handheld TV remote control. It was used on the AC-17 in a way similar to a remote: opening doors, turning lights on and off, and so on. Robinson knew that the remote had activated other devices in the past, things that it wasn't designed to work with, like iPods and laptops.

As the chamber door seemed to look so much like a garage door, he was hoping the remote sensing unit could help get it open. It was a long shot—and he knew it. But he hit the open button anyway.

At that same moment, there was a huge crash of heat lightning right above them. Meanwhile, as Gunn and the paratroopers were frantically looking for a weak spot in the tight doorway, one young paratrooper yelled in desperation, "What the hell is that phrase they say to open things up in this part of the world—from *1001 Arabian Nights*?"

Gunn overheard the paratrooper and yelled out, "Open sesame!"

His words came out at the same moment the heat lightning crashed above them and Robinson pushed the buttons on the remote control device.

And *whatever* happened—be it the remote, the lightning or Gunn's magic words, or a combination of all three—to the astonishment of all, the huge door suddenly opened.

THE insanity inside the tank went on and on.

Amanda was frantic now, twisting and squirming, but every time she moved, it only served to reinjure the wounded loader and paratrooper. She felt liquid running down her face. She was certain it was blood and that she'd been horribly wounded somehow. But when she wiped her cheek and then looked at her fingers, she realized they were tears and that she was crying.

About this time she heard Cardillo curse loudly, and then it was strangely quiet inside the tank. Cardillo had stopped firing his weapon—he was out of ammunition. So too was the driver.

Amanda froze. Everything just stopped. Then she heard QQB fighters swarm all over the tank. They were tearing at the hatches.

My God, she thought. *This will be my coffin . . .*

There came the sound of a tremendous explosion—Amanda was convinced the hangar of salt was coming down on them. Cardillo slumped into her arms—he was either dead or knocked unconscious.

Then she could hear more shouting, and the noise of the QQB fighters climbing back onto the tank increased. Then came a tremendous amount of gunfire, which to her horror she thought had to be the QQB killing the rest of the SSK fighters.

Then the most frightening sound of all. The top hatch in the turret was opening.

With supreme effort, Amanda shook the paralysis from her body and managed to reach into the injured paratrooper's boot and come up with his combat knife. If this was the QQB, she was determined to do them some damage before they took her and . . .

The hatch opened. The light flooded in. She held the knife tightly, ready to lash out.

But then she saw a smiling face looking down at her.

It was Gunn.

IT took a while to extract Amanda from the tank.

Cardillo had to come out first. He'd been knocked unconscious when a QQB fighter detonated a grenade atop the tank's turret, right next to Cardillo's unprotected head. He was revived with a shot of amphetamines from the 82nd Airborne's medic.

Next to come out was the wounded paratrooper. His legs were all shot up, but he was conscious. Same with the tank's loader. Injured but alive.

Gunn himself lifted Amanda out and, military discipline or not, hugged and kissed her deeply. She looked down at the tank and was horrified to see it was covered with blood and the bodies of QQB fighters. Then she realized what had happened. Gunn and the paratroopers had somehow opened the door and had come in shooting. Between them and the brave SSK fighters, they'd killed all the QQB fighters and had saved the day.

She climbed down off the tank to find all of the SSK fighters dead on the floor—except one: al-Kat. The paratrooper medics were working furiously over him. He'd taken a bullet to the head, they told her. It was iffy whether he'd make it or not.

She knelt down beside him and brushed the long hair from his face. He barely opened his eyes—and then managed a smile.

"Angel," he said.

Then a medic injected him with a massive dose of morphine and he went unconscious. Amanda said to the medic, "It's very important that this guy lives."

The medic nodded. "We'll try our best."

She joined Gunn again and they took a long look around the suddenly quiet mountain chamber. There was so much bizarre stuff in the cave it was mind-boggling. Again, lots of sneakers, lots of dead animals, lots of weapons. Lots of empty Adrenalin and morphine vials. But also a lot of women's clothing, and whips, and pot bongs and take-out food containers.

But as far as Gunn could tell, there were no nukes. None that he could see anyway.

The hangar was the largest space within the vast chamber. There were so many airplanes crowded inside, it was impossible to count them all. But, at that moment, Gunn would have bet his half of his $50 million reward that they had finally found the missing ex-Iraqi planes—or what was left of them.

But he had a surprise coming.

Captain Vogel came up to him and said, "You're not going to believe this, Major."

Gunn took off his crash helmet and just shook his head. "At this point, I'll believe anything."

Vogel led him deeper into the hangar

"You might want to modify that statement," the paratrooper CO told him. "Once you see what we've found."

Gunn was surprised that the hangar itself had sustained so little damage. Except for a few fires near the entrance, the smoldering rooftop and a few ceiling beams that had fallen, the hidden air barn was pretty much intact.

The paratroopers had spread out all over the hangar, which while crude looking and messy, held some fairly sophisticated machines and tools. It was also dimly lit inside and smelled of sour milk, animal fur and spilled aviation gas. And the place was absolutely overcrowded with jet fighters. In fact they were wing to wing, nose to nose for as far as Gunn could see.

"Did you do a count?" he asked Vogel, indicating the airplanes.

"We did—and are you ready for this?"

Gunn said, "I'm not sure . . ."

Vogel took out a piece of paper with some crude writing on it.

"We've counted them three times already, including some wrecks we found in that junkyard over there."

"And . . ."

"And they're all here," Vogel said.

Gunn shook his fist in triumph. "So we've found the rest of them—no more suicide planes."

But Vogel was shaking his head. "No—what I'm saying is they are *all* here. All *one hundred and thirty* of them."

Gunn just stared back at him.

"I'm not hearing you right," Gunn said.

Vogel showed him the rough list.

"They are *all* here," Vogel repeated. "All the Russian planes, all the French planes. One hundred and thirty of them. The *entire* ex-Iraqi air force *is* here."

Gunn was stunned.

"But how can that be?" he asked "There's been at least six suicide attacks, involving at least seven airplanes since this thing began. People *have seen* these airplanes carrying out the attacks. None of them survived. We just shot one down. And we saw two flying out of here. So how can they *all* be here?"

Vogel just shook his head. "I got no idea," he said. "But they are."

"Unless," Amanda said, joining them, "the suicide planes were coming from somewhere else. They would land here, they would change out the black boxes so the suicide plane *just looked like* an ex-Iraqi plane and then the original plane was destroyed. It was like a quid pro quo thing and the QQB guys just happened to be the right people to make the deal with."

The three of them thought about this. Even in this whole crazy adventure, that explanation sounded almost *too* crazy.

Yet, what else could it be?

"But if it's not the ex-Iraqi planes that are actually doing it," Vogel asked, "who is? Who wants to get Israel to attack Iran?"

"Who wants to end the world, you mean," Amanda said.

Gunn thought a moment. "Any chance there's anything left of the guy who just tried to take off from here?"

Vogel almost laughed. "He took a 122 shell right between the teeth," the paratrooper CO said. "I doubt his shoelaces are even still intact."

Gunn started to say something else—but stopped. He turned toward the open door and the outside world.

"Listen—hear that?" he asked.

It was a low roar at first—cutting through the sound of the wind and sand blowing around outside. But it grew and grew and soon everyone knew what it was.

"Another jet is coming in!" someone yelled.

"Maybe they know we're here and they're going to suicide bomb us?" Amanda asked.

"Everyone out!" Gun ordered.

The entire gunship team quickly exited the hidden chamber to see the lights of yet another jet fighter appear above the far end of the runway. It was an ancient MiG-21. It started its descent but quickly enough its pilot realized there was a huge airplane sitting at the end of the runway as well as at least one tank, plus a fire in the underground hangar.

It immediately tried to pull up.

Someone else yelled, "Shoot at it!"

Many people did. The paratroopers, the Marines—even Gunn and Amanda joined in with their sidearms.

The MiG went so slow overhead, trying to get some air under its wings, that it seemed to stand still for a moment. The people on the ground saw dozens of bullets bouncing off it, but a few of the rounds found their mark.

The plane seemed to stagger a bit. It was definitely wounded, but the question was, how much? It took a few seconds, but then its momentum began coming back and it started to increase in speed. One last desperate shot by the second Marine tank just barely clipped its tail section. The jet fighter was knocked off-kilter for a moment, and shook violently. But though it started smoking heavily, it regained its forward speed and began slowly flying off to the west.

Gunn yelled, "We've got to stop that plane!" And he was already running full speed toward the AC-17.

Amanda tried to stop him. "I *have* to go with you," she said.

But Gunn knew this had the potential to be very dangerous, and he had almost lost her just minutes before.

"No," he said. "You're staying here. I'll come back for you."

She started to protest, but he wasn't hearing it.

"Stay here," he said again. "And that's an order."

GUNN climbed up to the flight deck and quick-started the AC-17.

A dozen paratroopers jumped in with him, as did Robinson and his gun crew. The plane started rolling even before the hatches were closed.

The gunship roared down the runway, but with not enough power or momentum. It used the entire length of the rocky airstrip, yet still didn't take off. Finally, just before it would have smashed into the far end of the salt mountain, Gunn hit the rocket assists. The huge plane leapt into the air, going almost straight up.

It quickly gained altitude. Once it reached two thousand feet, Gunn turned west and the chase was on.

ONCE he was sure all his flight systems were fully functioning after the unconventional takeoff, Gunn turned on his air defense radar. At the very end of the first sweep, he saw a blip. It was moving west, flying at about fifteen thousand feet and going less than 120 knots.

"We may have put enough holes in him to slow him down," Gunn said to Robinson. He pushed his throttles full ahead and slowly started gaining on the MiG.

But what was he going to do next?

They needed this pilot alive—that was the whole point. But how do you take someone alive who wants to kill himself?

The MiG was indeed smoking heavily. The shots it had taken over the hidden base had exacted a toll. Gunn managed to catch up to the smoking fighter and give it the once-over. He knew for certain now that the plane was in trouble. Although the MiG could go much faster than the C-17, the fighter was faltering and barely maintaining its forward airspeed. Plus it seemed to lack almost all side-to-side movement. It was also obvious that the plane was not carrying any real weapons, as in cannons or air-to-air missiles. It was a very stripped-down aircraft, its own speed and gravity being its biggest weapon.

Gunn pulled up right beside the MiG, coming up on its right wing. He could see the pilot through the bullet holes in the gunship's windshield. The pilot looked over at Gunn, his face illuminated by the brightening sky. He was wearing a headband and a cloth across his face. But he had neither helmet nor oxygen mask on.

The MiG pilot glanced up and down the left side of the gunship. He saw the muzzles of sixteen huge weapons sticking out of its fuselage like cannon muzzles sticking out of a Spanish galleon. He seemed curiously indifferent to the fact that this huge, heavily armed plane was riding beside him. His demeanor seemed to say: Shoot me down if you want.

Then an idea came to Gunn.

How do you stop a person who wants to kill himself?

"Burn him," he yelled back to his gun crew.

They understood. They started firing incendiary shells from a Vulcan cannon, one round at a time. The desired effect was achieved in six shots. After that, the old MiG started to catch on fire. Crashing or being shot down was one thing. Burning to death was another. The suicide pilot couldn't take it for very long, the flames were creeping into his cockpit. Very reluctantly he blasted away his canopy and ejected. His chute opened as the MiG went down in flames, crashing into the desert below. The pilot started floating to Earth.

Robinson thought aloud, "Now what?"

Gunn only shook his head. "We've got to get boots on the ground to capture him. Or at least try."

Gunn yelled for his paratroopers to get ready; they quickly slipped into the plane's extra parachutes. Then Gunn did a wide circle, making sure he was right over the pilot as he continued descending. Properly set, he pulled the big plane up on its tail, yanked the engines back and lowered the flaps—it was an old trick. The plane seemed to stand still in the air, at least long enough for a dozen paratroopers to go out the back and drift down to the same area where the pilot had just fallen.

As it turned out, it was not too far from the K-22 air base.

CAPTAIN Vogel jumped with his troops.

Thanks to Gunn's perfect mimicking of Bada Bing's famous hover move, the dozen paratroopers landed just a few hundred feet away from where the suicide pilot had touched down.

As soon as he saw the huge American soldiers landing near him, the pilot started running. The terrain was hard and rough, with the rocky hills and many steep gullies that marked the western edge of the Dasht-e Kavir.

It took about ten minutes, and the help of the infrared searchlight on the AC-17, but finally the paratroopers spotted the pilot hiding in a sinkhole. He took off at first sight of them, but two paratroopers caught up to him fairly easily and tackled him.

Vogel was quickly on the phone to Gunn, letting him listen as it was happening. The paratroopers stood the pilot up and frisked him for weapons. He had none.

Then one of the paratroopers pulled off his face mask.

The rest of the troopers looked at the pilot and were shocked.

"Hey," one of them cried out. "He's not an Iranian!"

CHAPTER 18

Tel Aviv

The video clip was only about thirty seconds long.

Shot from a circling AWACS plane, it showed the Israeli Navy's nuclear-armed Dolphin submarine, on fire and sinking, while a rescue boat from a nearby U.S. Navy warship was picking up the last of its crew.

"I hope al Qaeda doesn't have any scuba divers on the payroll," Lieutenant Moon said, watching the sub slip, nose first, beneath the waves. "Then again, something tells me the fish in the gulf might be growing extra tails in a few years."

He clicked his mouse and went to another video just added to the CIA web page. It showed Bing's C-17ABL in pieces all over the extra-long runway at Khafji, Saudi Arabia.

Moon shook his head. "Let's see, that makes . . . what? *Three* billion-dollar planes the 201st has lost in less than a year? They might have a future in credit-swaps banking."

Newman was not paying attention to Moon's wise-cracks. He was still sitting at his desk nearby, poring over the Chinese satellite photos.

"We are missing something here," he kept saying, again and again.

Moon stayed at his computer this time, transferring the two videos to the local Israeli Intell site. He rarely received any acknowledgment for passing on these bits of information. The only intelligence bouncing back to him was that the number of nuke-armed F-15 fighter bombers waiting on Israeli runways was increasing by the hour.

Like Newman, Moon was overtired, his body locked in a perpetual state of tension that affected him from head to toe.

"When will this night be over?" he whispered. "Dear Lord, send us a sign . . ."

That's when Newman exploded out of his chair.

"Jesus Christ!" he exclaimed so loudly the Israeli analysts in the other part of the suite all looked up from their desks.

Moon quickly rolled his chair over to Newman.

"That's maybe not the name you want to invoke in this place," Moon cautioned him.

But Newman didn't care. He'd just made the connection that had been dogging him for hours.

"Look at these pictures," he urged Moon, holding up the photos of Russian planes flying in Turkmenistan that the Chinese had given them.

Moon groaned. The images didn't look any different from the last ten times he'd seen them.

"OK—so?" he finally asked.

"Now," Newman said. "Look at this . . ."

He opened his laptop and called up the mysterious "one flash" satellite photo that the CIA had used to send the 201st into the Dasht-e Kavir desert.

Moon looked at the image and then back at the Chinese photos—and suddenly he saw what Newman saw.

It wasn't what the photos depicted—it was the photos themselves. Both the pictures of the Russian planes and the one of the desert with the flash in it had the same distinct green tint around the edge.

"Ever see that kind of bordering before?" Newman asked Moon.

Moon had to shake his head no. He'd looked at thousands, maybe *tens* of thousands of satellite and intelligence photos in his career. He'd never seen ones like this.

They both just stared at each other.

What did this mean?

"Let's approach it rationally," Newman said.

He picked up a few of the Chinese photos. "We know these came from a PRC satellite—they told us so."

He picked up the CIA photo of the desert with the flash.

"This came from the CIA—yet they're *very* similar. What's the logical conclusion?"

"That the CIA got it from the Chinese—somehow," Moon said.

"Right," Newman said. "But the agency didn't want to tell us or anyone else *where* they got the flash photo, even though that PRC delivery boy had no problem giving us these?"

Moon thought a moment, then said, "And the Chinese have no idea we had the flash photo."

Newman nodded. "Exactly . . ."

Moon went on: "Well, that can only mean . . . the CIA must have a way to—what? Snoop in on Chinese satellite photos?"

Newman smiled for real.

"Well, wouldn't that be something," he said.

MOON was an expert hacker.

Newman had heard through the SOF grapevine that this was one of the reasons the diminutive officer had made it so far in the black ops world. It was also one of the reasons that he was always left to do his thing—with little interference or oversight from his superiors.

And Newman had seen this mastery at work. In his past association with the 201st, Moon had hacked into some of the country's most protected cyber-sites, including those belonging to the NSA and the NRO—arguably the most secret U.S. intelligence agencies in existence. Put simply, Moon could hack into anything.

Newman knew the fact that the Chinese satellite photos and the one the CIA had given them came from the same satellite meant only one thing: He and Moon were on to something here. It was also one of the reasons that he was always allowed to do his thing—with little interference or oversight from his superiors.

They closed the door to their office and for the first time in this long night, they went off the four-sided web page. Soon Moon's fingers were typing so fast it was almost comical. The pages flashing across his computer screen were moving at such a high rate of speed, they were just a blur to Newman's eyes. But Newman knew what Moon was doing—he was burrowing deeper and deeper into some of the darkest reaches of the U.S. intelligence community's security system.

All this was highly illegal, of course, and grounds for court-martial at the very least. But they were part of the 201st—such things had never been a hindrance before.

It took almost thirty minutes of nonstop typing—and at one point Newman actually had to dab Moon's sweaty brow, like a cornerman in a big fight—but finally the little intelligence agent accomplished what he set out to do: he broke into the CIA highly classified satellite photos archives.

"That was amazing," Newman told him

Moon just shrugged. "It's not that hard if you already know the codes," he replied enigmatically.

He spent the next twenty minutes flipping through thousands of top secret photo indexes until he found a series marked "Alternative Mandarin." It had a date stamp just a couple weeks old.

"Let me guess," Moon said, clicking on them.

Sure enough, they were a series of photos that all had the same greenish border, a slight emerald tinge that apparently showed up in all Chinese satellite photos.

"Our cousins at the agency have been working hard," Newman said. "Imagine being able to tap into whatever the Chinese satellites are looking at? I got a feeling Beijing would pull out all of its treasury bonds and shut down every Wal-Mart in the U.S. if they were aware of this."

Moon just nodded. "They would not be pleased, that's for sure."

The Alternative Mandarin file was gigantic—it contained tens of thousands of satellite photos, many of them close-ups of U.S. military bases, especially submarine bases, both on the continental U.S. and abroad.

A number of the photos in the file also contained pictures that the Chinese had taken over the Persian Gulf, and Iran in particular. Moon even managed to find the photo the CIA had given them, the one showing the solitary flash in the middle of the Dasht-e Kavir desert.

But there was nothing alarming or illuminating or even very interesting about what the purloined Chinese pictures showed. In many ways, they depicted nothing that Moon or Newman hadn't seen before. In other words, no smoking gun.

"Who would have thought the results would be so boring," Newman said, dejected.

Moon thought about this for a long time. Then he moved to the end of the Alternative Mandarin index. The last file was marked "Other—Domestic."

Moon knew the CIA had not reviewed these photos yet because none of them were time-stamped. The agency analysts probably didn't think there was anything worth seeing in them, but Moon opened the file anyway.

At first he and Newman had to agree. Most of the photos in this file were from Chinese satellites taking pictures of China itself.

There were thousands of photos in here too.

"But why?" Newman asked. "I can understand their satellites have to pass over their homeland occasionally—

but why take all these pictures? Or better yet, why save them?"

Moon thought about this too.

"Let's see what they're looking at," he said.

That's what they did for the next half hour, but again they were stymied. Practically all of the photos were of China's mining industry. Hundreds of pictures of mines, mine digging equipment, long and broad shots of country that presumably held mines underneath them.

"Why are they so interested in their own mines?" Newman asked. "I mean the only time you hear about them, it's because one has caved in."

Moon studied the photos again.

"Unless," he said, "these aren't really mines."

At that moment, Newman's cell phone rang. For a brief moment, he thought it might be his wife, but in the next, he knew that would be impossible. This was his secure phone.

"Who the hell is this?" Newman wondered, pushing the talk button.

As it turned out, it was Major Tommy Gunn.

"Colonel Newman," Gunn said. "You ain't going to believe this . . ."

AT exactly 0601 hours, Israeli time, the order to attack Iran was finally given.

The Israeli government told no one, not even the U.S., its closest ally, that the attack was on. Actually, there was no need to. Inside thirty minutes, the entire world would know what was about to transpire.

The order arrived first at a place called El Sira. This highly restricted facility located in eastern Israel was the closest Israeli air force base to the Persian Gulf. The first wave of the impending attack on Iran would be launched from here.

There were forty-two F-15K fighter bombers on the runways at El Sira.

The F-15K was a two-man version of the U.S.-built F-15E fighter bomber designed specifically for Israel's nuclear weapons delivery wing. Each plane was fitted with two tactical nuclear weapons to be launched by its two-man crew. Each plane had two primary targets to hit, and two secondary targets as backups.

The method of bombing was not overly complex. The pilots and plane wanted to avoid the shock wave and the intense radiation resulting from their bombs detonating, of course. That's why each F-15K carried updated smart bomb technology that allowed the pilot to approach his target from high altitude and release the bomb from as far as thirty miles away. This would allow his backseat weapons operator to guide it to its target from a safe distance.

The bombs would be dropped on primary targets like nuclear-processing plants, military bases, and population centers such as Tehran. Secondary targets like power plants and dams would also be hit. Precision was important but not critical. Each bomb contained seventy-two kilotons of nuclear destruction, exactly four times as much destructive power as the bomb dropped on Hiroshima. With that kind of kilotonage, accuracy wasn't really important. Just as long as the bomb got close to its target, the result would be the same: utter destruction.

The F-15Ks at El Sira had been warmed up and ready to go for two days now—only the pilots had changed. Sitting in the plane for ten- to twelve-hour shifts, the two-man crews had been relieved on a staggered basis, just in case the air wing had to go sooner than expected.

To get them safely to Iran, three squadrons of F-16 fighter jets were also warmed up and waiting in another part of the large El Sira base. They would serve as escorts for the attacking F-15Ks.

The combined force would be taking the most direct route to its target destination, basically a straight shot to the east. While this meant most of the flying would be done over air-friendly Iraq, on takeoff the strike force would have to cross into Syrian and Jordanian airspace for at least twenty minutes where they might be challenged.

But that's what the escorting F-16s were for.

WHEN the go code finally came to El Sira, the pilots and ground crews observed a moment of silence in order to say a quick Hebrew prayer together. Then began the final preparations for takeoff. Everyone involved knew there might not be much left—of this base or their country—once they returned, *if* they returned. The tension was as thick as the early morning fog covering the base.

The first F-15K rolled out and was ready to take off . . . when, oddly, the base's air raid siren began blaring.

Before the pilots or anyone else could absorb what this meant, a "runway fouled" alert also went out.

Incredibly, this meant that an unauthorized plane was landing at the base.

Being as restricted and secret as it was, El Sira was ringed with antiaircraft weapons, long-range early warning radar stations and even squads of Israeli soldiers positioned in the surrounding desert, watching for any incoming enemy aircraft.

Yet the plane in question had not showed up on radar, had not been spotted in the clear but still starry early morning sky, nor had its engines been heard by anyone at the very active base

What kind of plane is this?

Several hundred people at the base saw what happened next. One moment the base's main runway was clear and empty. The next, a huge airplane suddenly appeared out of nowhere—literally.

It hit the runway just seconds after materializing. Many of the Israeli pilots, while recognizing it was an American C-17, thought they were hallucinating or that this was some kind of psychological warfare. Perhaps the base had been hit with some kind of odorless, tasteless gas or bio-agent to disorient the pilots. Or maybe the drinking water had been compromised with psychotropic drugs.

In any case, the plane landed, its U.S. markings in full view, and eventually came to a halt. The base's security troops rushed out to the runway and quickly surrounded the big plane. The chief of staff of the Israeli air force, who was at the base to coordinate the first strike, also hurried to the scene. Was this an elaborate Trojan Horse plan by the Iranians to land here at Israel's most secret base? Or was this actually an American Special Forces aircraft of some kind with some fantastic technology involved?

No one knew.

The security troops armed their weapons and were prepared to fire. Their orders were simple: The top security officer at the base was sending radio messages to the unexpected visitor. He would give it thirty seconds. If he received no reply by then, the security troops were to open fire and destroy the plane.

The first several seconds passed by in surreal calmness. The F-15Ks were still moving to their takeoff positions, the mystery plane's intrusion holding up the nuclear attack by only a minute or so.

Fifteen seconds and counting.

The escorting F-16s began taking off over on the south side of the base.

Ten seconds—the security forces had brought up two enormous Merkava IV tanks. Their 122mm guns were leveled at the big U.S. plane.

Five seconds . . .

The security forces aimed their weapons

Four.

Three.

Two.

One . . .

And that's when Newman and Moon arrived.

THEY were riding in the car belonging to the top intelligence chief of all of Israel, a man whose activities were *so* classified, his name itself was a state secret. He was known only as Q.

His office was at Gideon's Circle. He had sped to El Sira at top speed with such sensitive news, he'd eschewed contacting the base either by phone or radio, knowing he would have to appear personally, if he was to be believed.

The car screeched to a halt just a few feet behind the rear of the mystery plane and the intelligence chief climbed out, along with Moon and Newman.

Q gave the airplane the once-over then whispered something to the base commander. This officer gave the order for the security troops to lower their weapons and stand down, but to also stay close by.

Then the man called Q turned to Newman and Moon and told them to tell the Israeli air force chief of staff what they had told him.

Newman did the talking.

"This plane is part of a highly classified U.S. Special Forces program," he began. "We cannot discuss its stealth technology. But we can tell you that it has just returned from a mission to identify and destroy the so-called suicide planes. I can also tell you that they were successful to the point of identifying who's behind all this—and that they can tell you unequivocally that the Iranians are *not* the culprits, meaning you must call off your attack. Or at least postpone it."

The chief of staff looked at the top spy, who just shrugged.

"They have all the credentials," Q told him in Hebrew. "I know it all sounds strange, but they've convinced me and we have no reason to doubt them."

Newman went on. "We know it sounds crazy. From what the people on this plane told us, we can go get the person responsible for all this, and be back here inside an hour. Just hold off your attack until then. We kept our part of the bargain—we found out who's behind all this—now it's your turn to keep your part."

The chief of staff had no idea what to do.

Finally he asked Newman: "Are you absolutely sure the people in that plane are on the level? That they've uncovered what every intelligence agency in this area has been unable to find out?"

"I stake my reputation on it," Newman said. "Let them out of there. You tell me your impression of them. Believe me, they are the tops."

The chief of staff finally relented. He gave a signal to his security officer who in turn motioned to the people inside the plane. In seconds, the big ramp at the back of the aircraft yawned open.

Judging from what they had seen and heard so far, those looking on expected a team of superheroes to walk out of the plane.

Instead, the first thing to come down the lowered back ramp was a herd of two dozen goats.

The chief of staff just glared at Newman and Moon. His face turned beet red. "What the hell is this?"

Newman and Moon were mortified.

They started to climb back into Q's car.

"One hour," Newman said hastily. "We'll be back before you know it."

THE high-speed ride from El Sira air base to Zuk Road back in Tel Aviv took twenty-five minutes.

Zuk Road was Tel Aviv's Embassy Row. This was

where many foreign consulates and diplomatic missions were located.

The largest building on the street was 22 Zuk. Newman and Moon had Q's driver pull up in front of this building and they got out.

The street was empty except for a small coffee shop on the corner. Newman anxiously checked his watch.

"Damn, we got about five minutes to do this," he told Moon. "Maybe we would have been better off using something other than a car to get here."

Moon just shrugged. "My spaceship is in the shop," he said without the slightest hint of irony.

They walked to the front door of the building, flashed their Mossad-issue security badges and were let in by the Israeli plainclothes guard.

They climbed on the elevator and went to the seventh floor. There was only one office up here. The diplomatic mission of the People's Republic of China.

They walked in without knocking. The spacious office was empty, with no overnight staff in evidence. They'd either been told to go home and be with their families on this long, dangerous night, or they had simply left on their own. In fact, there was only one office light on. Newman and Moon headed straight for it.

Deputy Ambassador Chin was surprised to see them when they appeared at his door. He was standing behind his desk, hastily packing a suitcase.

"Gentlemen?" he asked with much uncertainty. "I didn't expect to see you again so soon."

They walked into his office, at once struck by its size and ostentatious tackiness.

"We're on to you," Newman told Chin directly. "We know everything."

Chin's face went pale—sort of. "I don't understand what you mean," he said.

Moon walked across the room and stood right in front of the diplomat. They were approximately the same height.

"We know about the pilots and we know about the planes," he told Chin with chilling certainty. "And we know the planes are *not* originating in Iran. In fact, we know the whole plan. The mines. The sat photos. We know it all. Now all we need is for you to tell the Israelis before they blow up the Middle East."

Chin almost laughed at them. "I have no idea what you're talking about."

At that point, Newman pulled a massive handgun from his boot holster. Chin's eyes went wide when he saw the hand cannon.

"You think you're the only country with scary geniuses?" Newman asked him, pointing the gun between Chin's eyes.

Chin became nervous but he was not panicking—yet.

"Don't expect me to tell you anything," he began to bluster. "Nothing. Ever."

Moon shrugged. He was better at this sort of thing than Newman.

He walked across the office to Chin's bookcase. He examined the names of the various books, then punched one certain book titled *Modern-day Mining Techniques.*

The bookcase slid to one side to reveal a hidden room

behind it. Within were a couple dozen shelves all holding copies of the same bound document. Moon picked one up and showed it to Newman.

It was "The Falklands Factor."

Also in the hidden room were hundreds of DVDs and audio discs of speeches being given by various doom and gloom cult leaders. These had been popping up all over the world in the past few weeks.

"Interesting material you have here," Moon said.

"I thought freedom to read and listen to anything you want is a keystone of American democracy," Chin said, now sounding defiant. "If you think I'm guilty just because I'm doing the same thing as an average American, then you don't know who you're dealing with."

The remark made Moon's ears perk up.

The intelligence officer just laughed at him and said, "On the contrary, sir. *You've* got no idea who *you're* dealing with."

Newman looked over at the diminutive officer and felt a chill go through him. Again, Moon was a lot of different things: undercover agent, spy, infiltrator, saboteur, hacker—but Newman knew he was also a master interrogator. And if half the stories he'd heard about him were true, he was not of the touchy-feely variety.

This was a desperate moment—what happened in the next three or four minutes might decide the fate of the world. If they didn't get back to El Sira in time, Newman was sure the Israelis would launch their attack.

Newman saw Moon gazing at a pitcher of ice water sitting on Chin's desk. Even though he had known Moon for years, he really didn't know him well at all—and at that moment, he had no idea what he would do next.

The tiny officer turned to Newman and said, "Colonel, could you please close the door?"

Newman did as he asked. Then Moon produced a massive handgun of his own and forced Chin out from behind his desk. He made the diplomat lie on the floor, faceup. Taking some regular packing tape from Chin's desk, he bound him by the arms and legs. Then he wrapped a handkerchief around Chin's eyes and applied more tape, effectively blindfolding him.

Chin was horrified by now. He tried to cry out, but again, there was no one in the building to come to his aid.

Once Chin was bound, Moon shoved a couch cushion under his buttocks; this forced Chin's head back to the floor at an odd angle. Chin began to struggle but Moon brutally pistol-whipped him once across the face.

Then he shoved his head back, grabbed the pitcher of water and started pouring it down Chin's uplifted nostrils.

Newman was horrified once he realized what Moon was doing.

Waterboarding . . .

"Lieutenant?" Newman said tentatively.

Moon looked up at him calmly while Chin was gasping for breath. "Yes, Colonel?" Moon replied nonchalantly.

Newman was suddenly tongue-tied. It was a rare occasion that he didn't know what to say.

Finally he blurted out, "Will you need any help here? I was thinking of grabbing a coffee at that place down the street."

Moon calmly shook his head as he poured more water down Chin's nostrils. The man screamed for mercy.

"No, sir," Moon said. "It's all good here."

CHAPTER 19

Thirty minutes later

There were two unusual mobile trailers set up on the tarmac at El Sira.

They were bright silver and expensive looking. Both had been placed next to the huge AC-17 gunship. Just beyond them, the nuclear attack wing of the Israeli air force was still out on the runway, the 42 F-15K fighter bombers, engines still running, and pilots still in place.

The trailers' unofficial name was MSCPs, for mobile survivability combat posts. They were made of materials that protected the occupants against radiation and/or chemical weapons—for a while anyway. Their purpose? They would serve as a place from which to continue military operations once the nukes started falling.

One of the trailers was laid out as a medical unit, a sort of postmodern mobile army surgical hospital. Being treated inside at the moment were seven injured paratroopers, plus SSK commander al-Kat who was seriously wounded but expected to pull through. Amanda had been sitting at his bedside ever since they'd been allowed to leave the gunship. The Israeli army doctors running the place were all extremely attractive women and they too were paying a lot of attention to the Muslim fighter.

The next trailer over was laid out as a conference room, with a large table surrounded by all kinds of communications equipment. A strange mix of people was sitting around the table at the moment. Gunn was there, along with Bing, who'd just flown in from Saudi Arabia. Cardillo and Vogel were also on hand, as was a representative of the French Navy and a member of the Iranian Revolutionary Guards, looking very nervous to be actually *inside* the border of his country's sworn enemy. The man named Q was sitting at the head of the table; the Israeli air force chief of staff, and an additional gaggle of Israeli military leaders and politicians were on either side of him.

They were all waiting for Newman and Moon.

Just as their hour was about to expire, the door to the trailer burst open and the two Americans rushed in. With them was Deputy Ambassador Chin Li. He looked like he'd just lost a fistfight—underwater.

"Who is this man?" the chief of staff demanded to know. "And why is he all wet?"

Newman shoved Chin into the nearest seat. "He's your local PRC poster boy," Newman replied smartly. "And he tends to sweat a lot."

At that moment, Amanda walked in—and suddenly gave Moon an unexpected hug. The little intelligence agent was stunned. "What's that for?" he asked her.

"Because we never thought we'd see you again," she replied.

To which Newman looked up at her and said, "Where's mine?"

She smiled, hugged him and then took her seat next to Gunn. Everyone who had spent the night in the forbidding Dasht-e Kavir desert looked like they'd walked through hell and back—all except her. She looked like she was ready for another model shoot.

The chief of staff turned to Newman, and with no little aggravation said, "OK—it's your show. Explain to us why, number one, this soaking-wet Chinese man is here, and two, why I shouldn't give the takeoff order to my planes out there."

Newman looked at Gunn. Gunn in turn signaled one of the Israeli security guards standing nearby. He left the room briefly, returning with the pilot of the MiG fighter that Gunn had forced down earlier.

The mystery pilot had his face mask back on. He was forced into a chair close to Gunn but separate from the rest of the people at the table.

With no prompting, Gunn reached over and pulled the man's face covering off.

Then he said, "Gentlemen, this man is a suicide pilot."

And no, he wasn't an Iranian. He wasn't even from the Middle East. He was Asian. A gasp went through those assembled—then suddenly all eyes were on Ambassador Chin.

"Is this man Chinese?" the chief of staff asked of the pilot.

"No," Newman said. "Actually, he's Korean—North Korean."

Both the Israeli and the French representatives gasped

again. The Iranian diplomat was also astonished, but his face lit up considerably.

"You see now?" he said in broken English. "We were not involved. We did not plan these things. We did not carry them out."

Newman just nodded in the Iranian's direction. "I hate to say it, but he's right . . ."

Then he pointed to Ambassador Chin. "This man here did it all." More gasps.

"And here's how it worked," Newman went on. "This pilot might be North Korean, but don't be mistaken, there's no way those guys could have pulled this off. They don't have the IQ—or the fuel to fly halfway around the world. The only thing they could supply were airplanes, nutcases who could fly *those* airplanes, and the willingness to go on a suicide mission."

Newman rubbed his scruffy beard. "But knowing that, our friend here, Mr. Chin, and his comrades in Beijing, came up with a scheme right out of the old Mandarin days. They got the North Koreans to fly these suicide missions, using planes that are *similar* to the ex-Iraqi aircraft, just so the blame would be put on Iran. The Chinese allowed them to travel across China, get refueled a few times along the way, all with the intention of flying to the Dasht-e Kavir. Literally the middle of nowhere. Once there, they took the black box from one of the similar ex-Iraqi planes—MiG-21s and MiG-23s mostly—and put it into the North Korean plane, so people would think when they went through the wreckage that one of the ex-Iraqi planes had been used in the attack. The Chinese bought off these al Qaeda types, the QQB, who agreed that for every suicide plane that they helped come through, with fuel and the incriminating black box, they could rip apart and sell for scrap one of the *real* ex-Iraqi planes which Mr. Chin's associates in Tehran bought or, should I say, *stole* a few months ago. The Chinese knew that Israel would be frantic if they thought these suicide planes were going to attack them or even worse, nuke them, and that their reaction would seem to everyone like a prelude to a biblical Last Battle. All Mr. Chin and his friends needed then was for things to go haywire around the world—and they helped *that* along by spreading this bogus 'Falklands Factor' report crap everywhere and fanning the flames of this doomsday movement. And it worked, everyone started believing that, *shit,* Armageddon *must* be here. And as a result we started marching toward a doomsday war, thinking there was no way to stop it, when in reality it was just these PRC guys trying to knock over the first domino."

Moon added, "But they made three big mistakes. First, the Chinese had the North Koreans get involved because the North Korean's fly the same kind of Russian designs as the ex-Iraqi planes. But the ex-Iraqi planes also included French planes that the North Koreans *don't* fly—which we eventually noticed weren't being used. Again, Mr. Chin, that was your first blunder. Then, trying to get us to believe the Russians might be behind all this? That was his second mistake, because, sorry, the Kremlin just isn't that bright.

"But the third mistake was thinking that no one would actually go into that hellhole, the Dasht-e Kavir. Well, that was your biggest slipup of all. Because the people on that gunship did just that, and they're the ones who cracked this case."

Those assembled were simply astonished at the tale. But it sounded too implausible—too much like the plot of a cheap paperback novel.

"This is crazy," the Israeli chief of staff finally said. "How do you expect us to believe all this?"

Newman just turned and pointed to Chin.

"Just ask him," he said. "He'll tell you everything."

And to the amazement of all, that's exactly what Chin did. He laid out the entire plan, repeating it all, step by step, just as Newman had, including distributing "Falklands Factor" documents and having Chinese agents spread the doomsday rumors all around the world, but especially in the U.S.

But most chilling, he revealed *why* the Chinese wanted to start a nuclear war in the first place. Simply put, they viewed it as a means of population control.

"My government's plan was to put all of its key Communist Party members plus members of my country's 'useful population' into vast underground chambers prior to a nuclear war," Chin revealed, head bowed, speaking very low. "That's why we were always building mines and always having mine accidents. There was such a rush to get these things done. Once the war took place, these selected people, several million of them, would survive in these underground chambers, and emerge when the radiation settled down. The thought was that Earth would then be ours for the taking."

The group was appalled. Genocide by any other name was still genocide.

The French Navy representative asked Chin the question everyone had on their minds: "Even if your plan worked, billions would have been killed, but many of them would have been your own people."

Chin could barely speak now. "That's the inherent problem with China," he said. "Too many people. But we knew if we lost one half of our population, we'd *still* be one of the largest countries in the world—and one of the most powerful. With half our people gone, it would simply be more manageable, that's all."

"That's disgusting," Q said.

And everyone agreed.

Now came a long disturbing silence. Outside, the drone of the waiting jet fighters seemed to fade a bit.

Finally someone asked, "So what do we do now?"

That's when Moon piped up again.

"Anyone remember the movie *Fail-Safe*?" he asked.

CHAPTER 20

THE world finally exhaled.

Israel had "temporarily suspended" its plans to bomb Iran after receiving assurances that there would be no more suicide plane attacks. France and Iran agreed to immediately stop their little war. The multinational SOF groups hiding in countries surrounding the Persian state were recalled. And in its first true bombing mission ever, the Iranian Air Force obliterated the hidden base at the al-Kareet oasis in the Dasht-e Kavir. Less well known was the agreement to allow the SSK full immunity from the government in Tehran.

Other details had to be worked out, but for the moment, the planet was safe again. In mere hours, the doom-and-gloom rallies around the world started to peter out.

But there still remained the question of how to punish the Chinese for what they'd been planning. The people gathered in the silvery mobile trailer on the runway at El Sira discussed many options while keeping important capitals like Washington, Tel Aviv, Paris and Tehran in the loop.

To attack China outright would simply cause the nuclear catastrophe that everyone was trying to avoid. It was agreed that North Korea itself was beyond punishment; trying to hurt it somehow was the equivalent of kicking a corpse in the head.

Everyone agreed that Beijing had to pay.

But again—how?

"In the movie *Fail-Safe* a US B-52 bomber mistakenly nukes a city in Russia," Moon had explained to the group at one point. "To prevent an all-out nuclear war, the U.S. president agrees to allow Russia to drop a nuclear bomb on New York City."

From that simple explanation, a solution was finally found to make China pay for its disturbing transgression.

The job of doing it naturally fell to the 201st.

ACCORDING to Deputy Ambassador Chin, the vast underground chambers being secretly built by his government had cost more than a trillion dollars. There were four sites in all, virtual underground cities equipped with vast dormitories, food growing equipment, air filtration systems, fuel systems, water systems, road systems, hospitals, schools, even lakes. Supercomputers held all the secrets of Chinese industry and manufacturing. Special lighting systems were timed to simulate the sun, dimming in the "morning," getting bright at noon, and then dim again as "night" fell.

And like another old movie, tens of thousands of the most attractive Chinese women had been selected to be brought to the underground cities for procreation purposes.

Again, the Chinese hierarchy thought they could emerge from their underground lair in about ten years.

If they wanted to, that is.

THE bomb was nicknamed Super Blue.

Its real name was the GBU-43/B. Thirty feet long and forty inches around, a Super Blue carried a gigantic warhead containing nearly nineteen thousand pounds of H6, an extremely powerful explosive that could level a small city. Basically, the weapon was a nonnuclear, nuclear bomb.

Super Blues were also smart bombs as they could be guided to their targets by laser beams. They were also multipurpose. Clearing massive landing zones for helicopters was one good use. Taking out hardened targets was another. For a pure intimidation factor, they could be dropped during a war just to freak out the other side, because when a massive ordnance air blast went off, it produced a mushroom cloud that was almost indistinguishable from a real nuclear explosion.

They were also perfect for destroying underground chambers.

At the moment, the AC-17 had eight of them in its cargo bay.

* * *

THEY took off at sunset with all hands on board. The two M1 tanks had to be left behind because they'd both been damaged. But that just made room for some extra fuel bladders placed inside the gunship's cargo bay.

The plane went through aerial refuelings over Iraq, again over Iran and a final time over Pakistan. After the Pakistan top-off, the crew airdropped MREs on a small village in northern Pakistan inhabited by members of a small Muslim sect called the Cheshtiya. These people, whose ancestors had inhabited the same village for nearly two thousand years, had helped the 201st during its first adventure. Being perpetually poor and malnourished, the load of MREs would go a long way in helping them remain in their little piece of the wilderness, fed and safe, at least a little while longer.

While doing this, the AC-17 passed the mountain known as Bora Kurd. This was where the 201st had fought and defeated the dreaded Pashkar-e-Daku terrorist group in their first mission—the mountain where Gunn had fired all the AC-17's weapons at once, unintentionally blowing off the top of its peak. It now looked like a volcano.

From Pakistan, they flew into Chinese airspace. It was nightfall by now and the sky was appropriately full of stars. The AC-17 was basically retracing the steps it had taken to get to its first mission, flying over China, unseen and unnoticed, except this time going in the opposite direction, west to east.

No one saw them coming—not that it would have made much difference. The student pilots at the Chinese air force base at Quing Jang might have sensed an intruder violating their airspace, but there was nothing they could do about it, because as someone once said, "You can't stop what you can't see."

So too it was with the former residents of the village of Zhua Gong. They'd been forced to give up their family land for the greed of the central government to build a dam that would in just a few years fail and devastate the countryside. Had they seen the ripple moving across the stars, though, they would have interpreted it as a sign from the cosmos that better things were coming their way.

And then there was the young boy from a village near Keifeng, who, just a few months before, had thrown a rock in the air only to have it come back and hit him on the head. Having no idea that it had bounced off one of the invisible 201st C-17s passing very low overhead, he too would someday come to consider it a sign from above that things would not always be like this, that someday, his country would change.

The first two bombs were dropped on the Xianag Mine and a place called Giang Feng Cavern, both in west-central China. Literally rolled out the back, the bombs were steered to their targets by Gunn using the AC-17's weapons controller.

Bombs 3 and 4 fell the same way on a place called Yang Tang located in central China. Bombs 5 and 6 hit the Bung Dung caves—just south of Beijing. The last two bombs hit a place called Tung Bo, not sixty miles south of the Beijing itself.

The AC-17 flew right over the Chinese capital—not seen, not heard. The government leaders, in their mausoleums below, had little reaction to the reports that their underground utopias had all been obliterated by an aerial attacker no one could find. One phone call from Deputy Ambassador Chin had made it clear there was no alternative to just sitting there and taking it. The only caveat was that all of the vast underground sanctuaries had to be evacuated before they met their demise. The civilized peoples of the world didn't want to, in any way, aid in any Chinese population control efforts.

So the Communist Party's propaganda arm served up the spin that, yes, these were, in fact, mining accidents—huge ones. Then they immediately clamped down on news coverage of the accidents, hoping they'd eventually just fade away.

But behind the scenes in the ruthless Beijing hierarchy, heads literally rolled.

ONCE out over the Pacific, the AC-17 continued flying into the starry night, even though it should have seen the dawn a long time ago.

Gunn looked out at the stars through his windshield, picking out constellations and star formations that he knew were being sensed by the millions of diodes imbedded in the skin on top of his airplane and re-created by the millions more on the bottom.

But at the moment, it seemed like the sky was ablaze with ten or twenty times more stars than usual.

"It's weird," he said suddenly to Amanda, riding in the copilot's seat beside him.

"What is?" she asked.

"Well, this whole thing," he replied. "The ex-Iraqi airplanes, those planes in the desert. Israel being so hopped up to end the world. The Chinese egging them on, though they would have got the worst of it, as we would have. And those SOF guys from all over Europe? How were they going to attack the place the suicide planes were coming from? None of them even had helicopters. Deaf goats? These crazy guys in the desert? And who the hell picks up pieces of metal in the desert for a living anyway?"

"So?" she said.

"So, it seems very strange," he said, looking over at her radiant face. "It's almost like I'm still back in the penthouse, dreaming it all."

Amanda just winked at him and smiled.

"Maybe you are," she said.